Silver's Threads

Book 4

Other Titles by Penny Reilly

Silver's Threads Series

Book 1, Spinning Colours Darkly
© 2012 First Edition
© 2013 Second Edition

Book 2, Grey Weavings
© First Edition 2012
©Second Edition 2013

Book 3, Warp and Weft
© First Edition 2012
©Second Edition 2013

Forthcoming 2014

**Silver's Threads Book 5,
Skeins of Tyme**

Silver's Threads

Book 4

Silken Web

Penny Reilly

I dedicate this book

...to a dream of our beautiful planet at peace and a human race that holds her above all else;

...without her we have no physical home...

...and to Sandi and Sara who both left this world
...safe travels in the between sisters...

Special Acknowledgement

The beautiful cover art of this book "Dew Drop Dawn" is by the extraordinarily gifted Josephine Wall. I am honoured to work with her creations …her art has constantly inspired me through the birth of 'almost' five books; her paintings come to life for me as I write, whispering their magickal stories; I only hope my words can do justice to her art.

Please visit Josephine Wall on …her face book page…

www.facebok.com/TheOfficialJosephineWall

Support the artist, visit her Gallery and buy her beautiful art at…
www.josephinewall.co.uk

Acknowledgements

No book is born without the aid of family, friends, colleagues and ultimately, readers …on all counts you know who you are. I thank you deeply for your support and for your faith in me to get the job done…

…blessings to all …Penny

Foreword by Penny Reilly

Although my books to date are in the category of fiction, where does fiction end and inner experiences become truth, become reality. Where do fiction and myth, crossover? How much do we influence our world through our thoughts and dreams and through the direction of our will? 'Where your mind goes energy flows', is what I am attempting to express through this series.

As I began this book, I realised how much of me is in all of them. A greater part of me is the wild child Alma as much as the shapeshifters and other characters, born of my inner meanderings and my search for understanding through the years. If we believe something is, then indeed we are the co-creators of its birth.

The metaphorical journeys of the characters in this series are a taste perhaps of what humans are capable. What is attainable when they let go the fear of change or the unknown that holds them in thrall. Through a series of belief systems, they may have embraced, less than the ideal family values and ties, friends, teachers and peers. All these learned patterns can be our undoing unless we can identify what our own beliefs are or what is ingrained, 'picked up' so to speak in the growing years of childhood, also dependent on the environment of those years.

Each of my characters has a strong intellect but no less a strong belief in other realms of being, whereas so many a, 'if you can't see it with physical eyes it can't exist', attitude. I say to people of this nature '…you can see the trees move but you can't see the wind'. I challenge you to follow the threads of your own lives and ancestry, not in a linear direction but in a widespread, far-reaching continuum, for I truly believe nothing really dies, merely changes form.

…blessings …Penny

CONTENTS

...the story so far

The warp and weft of the threads of time begin to unravel, as seemingly random events bring the group closer together and yet geographically, spread further apart; new energies have joined the quest to find Sybille.

The Greenman Ways store opened at Samhain in the UK, Beltane in Australia and the group travelled the Between, to help with the set up. This keeps them all on their toes as the search for Sybille and now for Nina, continues. They find methods to travel the Between, whether they can shape change their skin or not. Tara, Claire and Lily, are helping where they can. Susan has re-discovered the pathways of old through her paintings and has created a portal from her studio, with a painting hung in Greenman Ways in Glastonbury.

New members of the group arrived, Vanessa, Annie Savages' daughter; Jamie, fox shapechanger, who has a history with Maeve in the Skeins, yet to unravel. Robert, an old friend and High Priest who worked with Sybille, both professionally and Magickally… who knows where he might fit as the search continues.

James has further knowledge to reveal. Quiet Cal, given a vision by Hercurin that will change the outcome of many things, is sworn to secrecy until the right moment to reveal it.

Sam experienced huge trauma whilst joining with her aspect Magdalena, as she burned alive as a Wytch; they are now one being, as are Annie and the ancient La Stregga who is attempting to awaken Annie from her intolerant arrogance. La Stregga is trying to compensate for her own unforgivable misdemeanour of oath breaking, in the fear for her own safety that revealed Magdalena. She dies as Magdalena burns, slamming though the veil into Annie, reuniting them as one. Aelish has no mercy for their mutual weaknesses.

Bethan has more questions as to how her mother died and what part her Fae father, Aithlin has yet to play in the tangled threads. Aerandir has agreed to help find out more as he too attempts to make sense of his fiercely competitive and arrogant mother Aelish, sister to Aithlin.

Within all this, Sybille has still to be found and the blight that threatens the realms of the Fae are becoming more visible to the increasingly sensitive group.

...the story continues

Silken Web

Willows bend and sway with ease
Many kin feel her dis-ease,
A chorus of sound, as mortal pleas
...pluck the Skeins of Tyme

Who hears the call and follow must,
With harm to none, fair and just,
The clarion cry for love, for trust
...vibrates the Skeins of Thyme

Each colour a note, a sound vibrating
Within each sound, a memory, waiting,
To reveal, new life awakening
...upon the Skeins of Tyme.

Sweet, discordant, flat or sharp
As the notes wrung from a harp
Such songs lie, 'neath each beating heart
...upon the Skeins of Tyme

...Arianwen Isil'Lindir & Aithlin Farandir
...From the Skeins of Tyme

# *Prologue*

...moon tides turning... fires burning
...winds blow cold across the land
...inner dreams and visions glowing
...bringing warmth to cold, cold hands
...winter's darkness, now approaches
...creeping closer on tiptoe
...go within to seek the silence
...move in the cycles... ebb and flow

Samhain on Tor Hill, where the group gathered in the frosty air, wreathed in mist and silence. Tara and Morgan moved fast to catch Samantha before she hit the ground. Flora, standing in front of her, heard a muffled groan, a smell of acrid smoke suddenly bitter in her mouth, as she turned to see Sam disappearing into the Between.

For Sam, it was as if the dark earth of Samhain's wild hunt broke loose to swallow her. Tara and Morgan moved as one, diving into the Aethers to follow her flight, dragging her back from the edge.

Bethan gathered the others close around her. Robert, Alex, Max and Cal turned instinctively, their backs to the gathered women, to create a protective circle around them. No one else apparently witnessed the incident, but it was not for 'Onceborn' eyes. Bethan's change came fast; eyes flashing with an otherworldly light, she sought to penetrate the darkness, while shielding the group from those waiting to burst from the hill in the ride of the Unsidhe.

Winds rose, howling, drawing the attention to a figure that stood, from another era. Small and slight, her dark hair blowing across her face, she raised a slender hand to Vanessa, who saw her manifest from within the hill but knew she was no Fae. Recognition dawned from her shared dreams. 'Nina!' She called softly but the apparition vanished and before they knew what was happening Jamie was gone too, changing rapidly to his canid form. He had been alert for this signal to get Nina out of danger. She would begin a new life under Nangini's tutelage.

Morgan carried Sam and Bethan ushered the others down the hill to Greenman Ways, where they enfolded Sam in a cloak of protection. Flora administered the antidote to the herbs Sam mixed for Magdalena, before they took hold in her own physical body. Tara alerted them; Sam did not share the fact that she must kill her own aspect in order to bring her to the same thread to merge. No one could have ever expected it would be like this.

As they struggled to hold her writhing figure down, Sam's hair smoked, her skin seared raw, blistered. As they dragged her back from the brink of the void, for a brief moment Morgan saw her shift a little; only for a second, but long enough for him to see dark feathers merge with leaves and flames. Words came to him from her message from Sybille all those months ago… *Earth you are, from earth you came, your intellect from Air you gain, your Fire should burn, with flaming ire yet Water has put out your fire…* and then the sprites were there, soothing her burns with their leafy sap, singing a song of shifting change. Forgotten was the Samhain Rite.

Chapter 1
Darkness Prevails

...in the blink of an eye we're gone from here
...to play in the breeze that blows away fear
...as the west winds howl and the piper calls
...we follow in the dance, held in Her thrall
...on we dance to the sound of music so sweet
...swept on in the rhythm of Her pulsing heart beat
...through the realms of night into brightest day
...'til we reach the Summer-country
...on the Crooked Path's Way
...where our tears are dried and the pain is done
...we dance on again, laughing, for we're free, we've won
...though we're battle weary, we fear no harm
...for the piper's trill calls us
...to the Mother's waiting arms

(Written and dedicated to Sandi Allen)

Sam flew through the Aethers, unfettered, free of all human burden and pain. A cool, fragrant wind, ruffled long flight quills, all memory gone, of who or what she was, had been or ever would be, in that moment. Carried under a cloak of musky-sweet feathers; safe, a gentle recall emerged of warm arms and soft down.

Then, something was pulling at her, tugging at her mind insistently; 'Sam,' she heard. 'Sam, come back, it's not your time to leave.'

An acrid odour seared her nostrils; offensive, as burnt feathers or hair and she fought to maintain her blissful flight away from the realms of pain and dark matters.

A voice grew stronger, this one deeper, a masculine melodic tone; Morgan sang to her, calling her back…

Life is a struggle when we see through the veil… hands become fragile; skin fair and pale. Come home from the dreaming… come back to this place, now's no time to travel, come home from this space.

You are a dreamer, one who sees true… memories awaken …feather's blue-black hue. Free flying… falling… then higher you soar, come home from your dreaming… there is more… so much more.'

Tara cast Morgan a sidelong glance, surprised by his remembrance from within, a song his kin would have sung to him somewhere in the deep dreaming of the Between; his father, perhaps, but no, Pwyll was listening with a small frown on his face but no sign that he recognised the words.

Where had it come from? Tara thought quietly to herself; wherever it had, worked. Sam stirred, groaning in reawakened pain, coughing harshly, the memory of her lungs full of choking smoke returned. She fought to stay gone from the memory, but the soothing sounds of Morgan and Tara's voices calling her back insistently, were undeniable. She felt her head lifted into a soft, feminine lap and the fragrance of forest flowers washed away all trace of the acrid smoke she could smell and taste.

Bethan, she thought, muttering hoarsely, 'Bethy,' before tears found her, coursing down her cheeks unchecked as the group assembled around her to touch gently, stroke and caress and to share their pain for her in a silent wash of grieving. She opened her eyes briefly just once to meet the soft grey-eyed gaze of Max Fenner, his concern palpable and his memory clear.

Great Goddess, he thought, how could I have been so weak to have let her burn, as he remembered the young maid Magdalena, his love for her and his ultimate betrayal. He wondered in a moment of panic what had become of his daughter Nina; Max closed his eyes in pain, willing the memory simply to go away and that Eduard Grimaldi, not be his aspect.

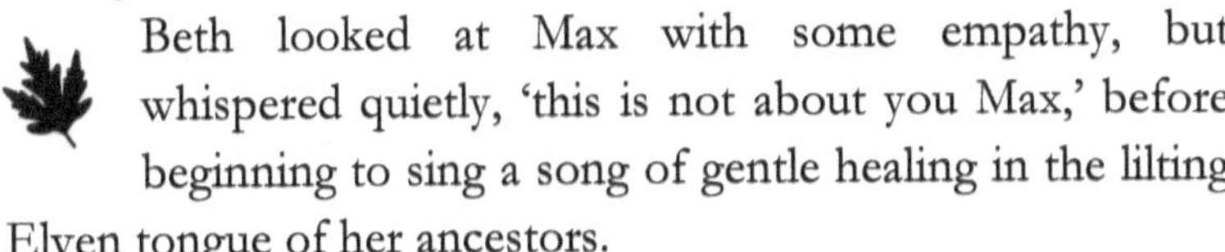Beth looked at Max with some empathy, but whispered quietly, 'this is not about you Max,' before beginning to sing a song of gentle healing in the lilting Elven tongue of her ancestors.

Through her song, Sam transported to a forest glade where sunlight filtered through a canopy of trees and a piper played a muted melody of blessing, slept. Small leaf sprites worked anew on her body, flames and feathers accompanied the leafy vines and blossoms, previously displayed on her skin and still she slept.

Chapter 2
Awakenings

...layers of awareness awakened by our dreams
...consciousness hindered by the 'doing'
...plans and schemes
...if we could simply let the 'now'
...become our journey's theme
...then we would soon discover, not the 'how'
...but what 'being' truly means

From that moment on, everything changed. With the Rite incomplete on their thread in the weave, the friends, made harshly aware of the seriousness of what had happened, whilst they tried to make sense of the obvious influences their far-reaching aspects had, within the Skeins of Tyme. All they yearned for was to bring Sybille home and restore their lives, although none of them even considered anything ever being as it once was.

They left Sam to sleep cradled in friendship, her head in Bethan's lap and attended by Tara. Quietly, they exchanged looks at Morgan's tender care of Sam, speaking sotto voiced; sharing opinions, wondering exactly what had happened to Sam to put her in such a state.

Flora spoke up in her practical way. 'It's not for us to speculate is it?' she said with some force. 'Sam's been having the dreams of Magdalena's death for a while and feared their eventual bonding would mean she relive the event, the violence and pain of her death. We should be more concerned about why this is, in the first place. What has happened in the Skeins that caused such an aberration?' She broke off, turning to Cal for comfort in his arms.

He held her gently, speaking to the room. 'Sam's obviously linked completely with Magdalena now, but it remains to be seen how she'll cope with the duality of it. We can only guess what she's going through, be there to support her in any way we can.' He turned as Bethan came into the room.

'We most need to consider why any of these events are occurring and how they're linked to Sybille's disappearance wouldn't you say?' she said forcefully, echoing Flora's words. 'As we well know, nothing happens in isolation. Somewhere, somehow we're all involved. Through forgotten acts, thoughts or meddling, we've instigated it all, directly or by our aspect's actions. We need to talk this through. Cal can you contact everyone to call them here from Glastonbury by our sundown tonight, no exception. I know Lily is flat out, but we need her here too; it's easy for her to shift through the veil.' An aura of power throbbed around her as Arianwen manifested briefly, to underscore the importance of the simple words spoken.

'I'll go get her,' said Morgan, coming out of Sam's room. 'Sam's sleeping more peacefully now and Tara's going to stay with her.'

'No need to shift Mor,' said Max. 'I can call her; we've developed almost a telepathic link recently.'

'What about Maeve?' said Flora, 'James too. I feel he has an important role to play. Oh, and that lovely man Robert Cromlech too; Tara said he would be joining the Grove.'

'Apparently, he can't travel long distances,' interjected Alex. 'He has some sort of condition.'

'Well, perhaps we should all travel there, then,' replied Beth.

'What about Sam?' said Flora. 'We can't leave her here alone; Tara has to come too.'

'Tara and I can get her through,' replied Claire. 'She weighs nothing now, which is a concern in itself, but yes, she needs to be with us and…' she broke off in surprise as Morgan interjected.

I'll take Sam through,' said Morgan with conviction, 'then you two are free for other things.'

With a nod of agreement and a raised eyebrow at Tara, who grinned mischievously, Claire continued without commenting on his statement. 'I think you're right Flo. Maeve, Robert and James need to be there, but how do we contact James or Maeve, come to that?'

'I have his number; I'll call him,' said Beth.

They agreed to travel together on the Aether, after they finished their daily tasks, later that day. Beth returned to sit with Sam; Morgan trailed in behind her.

Chapter 3
Morgan

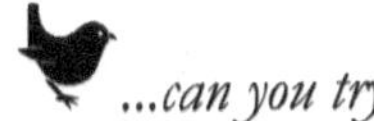

...to break the shackles binding flight
...when dreamless sleep's enfolding halts the fight
...can you fly?

Siting by Sam's bed, Morgan had never felt so helpless. He could not work out what was niggling away at him. Something he missed before was bubbling to the surface and he would just have to be patient to see what would present. Calling quietly to his aspect, he waited for a sign that Bran heard.

He tried to recall exactly what he had witnessed as Sam went into shock; he heard her gut wrenching screams on the Aethers and arrived together with Tara. Her flight was another curious thing, she definitely shape-changed. Tara had seen but not acknowledged it in any way. Morgan was barely beginning to make sense of it as he linked consciously with Bran. Yet he had not figured out where Sam, fit in with Bran, Maeve and Beth or the Merrow either, just another unfathomable cog in the wheel.

Flora and Cal remained the anomalies within the group; they're not having discovered any direct aspect links. He thought Flora was the means by which Nina and Magdalena might find their paths, but where was Nina now, he wondered and how would she be coping with the harshness of Magdalena's death?

Cal was brilliant, always calm and together; his far-sight developing, he received more information about the discovery of the bird-woman's body, but they had yet to tackle Tara about where the shapers fragile remains were. Cal, full of ideas, seemed to be keeping something to himself. When Morgan questioned Cal about it, he said he was having dreams of being a young lad of a Celt tribe. His name escaped him, but his first memory was of out hunting for food and witnessing something terrifying that he fought hard to remember.

Then of course, there was Max he mused, as he watched Sam stir in agitation before falling into unconsciousness again. They knew, after Cal's far seeing that Eduard was Max's aspect. Morgan felt intuitively the pain of Sam's experience linking her back to Max, who remained stubbornly silent about his own dreams; at least he appeared free of the Merrow's influence. He professed that if he spoke of it, it would become manifest.

His own sister Lily was so busy with the new store he'd not had much time to engage with her on the matter, but knew she was as always, solid as a rock. She seemed to have come to terms with Pwyll's unexpected appearance but made no mention of their missing mother.

Beth and Tara left the room briefly. Morgan did not notice the glances they exchanged as they observed his deep, internal meanderings.

Sam stirred, muttering something unintelligible; the sprites, agitated by her raw pain, became fierce in their protection, lifting like a shining green cloud from her writhing body. Sam struggled to stay manifest, appearing to morph in and out of sight; they challenged Morgan, then seeing who it was, they returned to tend Sam lovingly. Several remained, coming closer to look searchingly in Morgan's face, their little thorn swords pointed at him.

Morgan did not flinch when they moved closer still; so close he could smell their honeyed fragrance; he stayed still hardly daring to breathe.

In silent agreement, they moved in a sudden whirl of activity, he felt tiny pinpricks of dull pain but only briefly. His long hair lifted from his shoulders as their wings caused a breeze of perfumed air. Tugs at his scalp, followed by more sharp pricks of almost pleasurable pain, lulled him into a meditative state. Now I know how Sam feels, he thought in wonder. The tugs and pricks continued until his senses were so dulled he fought sleep. Just when he felt his head begin to nod forward, they stopped. Without a backward glance, the sprites returned to Sam and the rest of their tribe.

He turned as the door opened and Tara came back in. She stopped in her tracks when she saw Morgan, almost losing herself to mirth as a giggle bubbled; smothered quickly with her hand. She merely lifted her eyebrow in a knowing look before sitting by Sam again, stroking her forehead with a loving hand and soothing both Sam and her sprites with murmured words of encouragement.

Morgan realised he could understand every word. He rose and stretched limbs, cramped from sitting in one position for so long, stunned to find an hour was gone since Bethan and Tara left the room.

Walking to the adjacent bathroom, he splashed cold water over his face, reaching for the towel he, glanced in the mirror and froze. The sprites had twisted portions of hair into dreadlocks. A raven feather hung from a braid that pulled one side of his heavy fall of hair away from his face; it revealed half his forehead, covered in an intricate tattoo of feathers, flames and leaves, mirroring Sam's exactly. He could only stare, as the images appeared to writhe on his skin before disappearing, reappearing again as he focused in on the detail. He felt honoured by the decorative work of the nature sprites that were so loyal to Sam, but trepidation at the prospect of what the flames could mean. With a sharp intake of breath Morgan straightened, drawing his shoulders back, lifting his head stoically to face what was still to come for them all. At that moment, he shifted from changer-Cunningman to the warrior, the tattoos on his face adding a maturity and purpose to his striking features.

Chapter 4

 *Callum*

...through death and change our awareness grows
...as spring blossoms bright and winter snows
...blow howling gales through our empty heart
...still, we wait to realise our part

Cal grew up with the strange feeling that he kept a secret close to his chest. Deeply buried, it struggled to rise to the surface; a memory, stirring with a sound akin to the low buzzing of bees, he'd heard since Hercurin made him promise to keep secret the knowledge shared before Beltane. He could not work out why he was the one singled out, other than his undeniable sense of loyalty and duty to the Forest Lord, who was impossible to refuse. He knew this was something important that would reveal itself in due course, something to link all the previous events together, including Sybille's disappearance.

He never used to fret at things he did not understand. He only wished the nagging feeling of something impending would go away, vowing to speak to Tara again about the body he found on the Wolds. She was evasive in her reply to date. Suddenly the idea hit him that, with the recent development in his ability to far-see, he could take some time to scry the Wolds, tracing the trail Tara and Lily followed when searching for the vanished bracelet.

Gardening always soothed his senses. Making his way to the greenhouse, he checked the tomato seedlings alongside their companion plant, basil. It seemed unusually quiet in the garden; a pall of fine dew droplets covered everything and an unusual, if mild, chill in the air for the time of year had him raising his shirt collar over the back of his neck.

Two charcoal grey Gang Gang parrots flew screeching, low overhead; red faces a bright flash of sudden colour, they called the storm sure to arrive before the day was out. One paused, floating on the current of air just above Cal's head; he was sure it spoke, 'beware, beware,' before flying after its mate with a dip of elegant wings. Cal found himself saluting in respect, catching himself with a grin of derision. 'Thanks,' he called aloud to them, as they disappeared over the forest edge.

Walking into the greenhouse, his cheerful grin slipped from his face. Swallowing hard as his gorge threatened to rise, he stopped dead. Small Fae figures, birds and little creatures, possum, mice and tiny pygmy bats hung suspended in sticky webs from the roof beams and draped across the shrivelled seedlings he and Flora, had so lovingly raised from seed. A sound of buzzing insects recalled his memory of another thread in his personal tapestry; one he rarely spoke of, in truth only Claire and Flora knew.

He stumbled, reeling under an onslaught of images as he stood again in his father's library. His father's body hung suspended by a rope, twitching in the death throws apparently inflicted by his own hand

Cal remembered, what felt like running in slow motion. He stood the upturned chair and climbing on it, lifted his father's body high enough, with a strength born of terror, to loosen the deadly bindings from choking him further. He knew instinctively that this was not by his father's own hand. There was no reason known to man, why Richard would attempt to end his own life; this was not his debonair father's style at the peak of his remarkable career. There was no way given he would leave his son in this brutal fashion, no matter what else may be happening in his psyche since the death of his much loved wife, Cal's mother. As it happened, his father never recovered physically from the shock and never spoke again, other than to say as Cal cradled him, waiting for the medics to arrive, 'I didn't Callum, you have to believe me I didn't do this,' before lapsing into an unconscious state.

'What… who did this,' Cal remembered yelling to his father as he received mental images of dark threads of sticky webbing, covering the ceiling where his father hung suspended. Richard was never able to tell him what happened. During his comatose state, he suffered a massive stroke, which robbed him of speech and sight, tragically deleting all memory of his life and brilliant career, all but an unfinished paper that Cal was working on, days before finding the ancient bones on the Wold.

Now he knew exactly what had happened to his father. With a surge of pain, he fell to his knees, tears coursed unchecked down his face.

As his sight cleared enough to see around him, he realised that the sun was out, the greenhouse untainted by the ghastly, rigid dead creatures and Faefolk, the scent of tomato vines clean in the air.

Slender, muscular arms came around from behind to hold him while he let go the tears held in check for his father for three years. Richard McIntyre sat in his chair in the nursing home Cal had found; forced to place him there for the necessary full time care. His strong, elegant and wonderful father might just as well have died on the day he found him hanging It would have been kinder but Richard held on until his life drained away. He rallied on Cal's last visit to say simply, 'look to the darkness in broken change…' and it was there, later that day a staff member found him in his last long sleep.

In the greenhouse, a low humming like bees was the only other sound, heard dimly through the harsh, gut-wrenching sobs of the man.

Chapter 5
Flora

Flora grinned as she watched Cal from the kitchen window, witnessing the interchange Between man and nature with fondness and a deep sigh of contentment that he was a part of her life, grateful too that she was no longer alone. She kept looking out as he moved into the greenhouse seeing the world grow dim when he opened the doorway.

Casting off the dish to shatter on the seasoned wood floor, she vanished out the doorway. A strange rush of sense experience, shrinking her already diminutive size gave her a different sense of spatial awareness, the world got larger, overcame her. In the sheer determination, she made the greenhouse as Cal fell to his knees; she performed what was instinctual to her nature and held him quietly, wordlessly, while he sobbed.

Cal recovered only slowly, requiring time to gather his thoughts into something cohesive. Flora waited, silently reading the man, the greenhouse and the layers of pain she experienced, through a witnessing of such strength. Unnoticed by either of them, small tracks appeared in the ground as a creature moved back from the scene, invisible to their eyes. Only the door as it banged shut, in the sudden gust of wind alerted them to the creature's presence; 'Merrow,' they said in unison as sly laughter whispered softly in their ears.

Flora drew Cal to his feet. 'Come on love, I'll get you some rescue remedy and a cup of something strong for your nerves. Do you want to talk about what just happened?'

'I think it may be time to talk to everyone tonight' he replied. 'I would rather sit with it for now and not have to repeat it twice, if you don't mind Flo?'

'Whatever you need,' she said, reminding him how strong and kind she was.

He held her murmuring softly. 'I'm so blessed to have you in my life Flo'; he echoed her thoughts, of when she had watched him pause to speak to the bird, it seemed like hours ago.

Cal shifted her tenderly, so he could look in her eyes, his glance straying over her face, taking in everything about her, as if committing it to memory. Stroking her hair to smooth the wayward curls, he pulled two tiny feathers buried deeply in a tangled knot. Flora yelped as Cal pulled them out, blood tipped the ends. He held them out to her as she rubbed her scalp, fingers coming away bloodied, her eyes opening in surprise and pain.

'It would seem I have something to inwardly digest and tell the group about too,' she said with a watery grin, taking the small brown and blue feathers from him. 

'Ah,' was all Cal managed to say before she kissed him thoroughly.

Closing the door behind them, Flora walked ahead while Cal, making sure he bolted it tightly to keep in the meagre warmth, paused again to look through the glass. A slender, elegant being, stood in the centre of the greenhouse, she was looking directly at him with a question in her eyes. She appeared to be gauging his response. A bow and a quiver of arrows were slung apparently casually over her shoulder, but he sensed they would be drawn in readiness at a moment's notice.

Cal made to open the door again; he did not like the look of her and once again heard the buzzing sound in his ears. He knew she had nothing to do with his vision, but that somehow the visions drew her to him; he sighed deeply.

'More riddles,' he groaned, before following Flora to the house, rubbing at a sudden sharp pain in the centre of his chest, he thought he felt a strange ridge of skin there as he rubbed but it disappeared quickly, almost before it registered.

He walked back in to find Flora and Vanessa on their knees, clearing up shards of coloured glass, Claire poured tea from Sybille's ancient teapot for anyone who wanted it. They drank in silence, glancing occasionally around as each saw in turn the encroaching blight as it crept into their very bones, freezing to the core.

Bethan found them there together. 'This feels more like Samhain than Beltane,' she said softly as her antlers rose from her brow and a sense of peace flowed over the silent group.

'Come on,' she said, 'we must remain positive or the dark will feed on our fears'

They had not realised how quiet it had become; static silence like before an earthquake or a major storm, as suddenly in the garden the birds began to sing again

'Well the birds never lie,' said Cal quietly. Lighting the candle in the centre of the table, he made a warding gesture to the darkening sky.

Chapter 6
Sybille and Nina

...deep within the fragile strands
...altered by Unsidhe hands
...halflings, mixed-bloods, contrabands
...their blight then spreads across all lands

Caught up in a veil of darkness that covered her eyes, Sybille was unaware of the danger to her physical body until she felt the bindings, invisible to human sight, around her ankles and wrists and worse, around her throat. Teeming numbers of Dark and Light Makers were battling for her physical body; the Dark to invade and sully, the Light to feed her starving form; she was little more than flesh and bone.

Her Aetheric self, hovering wraith-like close by was unable to make sense of the scene, all memory of her Trueshape, flown. She only remembered that she was searching for something... someone, who could give her answers and suddenly there she was, curled in a niche in the great Birthing Tree but too frail to help her now. With a sigh, she withdrew her searching song and slumbered again beneath the heart of a slender young woman who's Trueshape they shared.

Elsewhere, their Trueshaper Silver, ailing too from the onslaught of the Dark, was searching for the fallen Littleshape known to her as Sybille. It was imperative to reunite Aetheric and physical bodies before the physical became unable to operate without its 'animator spirit'. It would have become no more than a shell after all this time, assuming it survived at all. If that were the case, so much was lost and her own rendered form could only survive for so long with the missing aspect of her most advanced Littleshape, vanished. Silver drifted through the Aethers, ever searching, battling the light and dark within and calling for Sybille through the song that linked them.

She drifted on through the small village of Glastonbury, compelled to look again. One aspect still tugged at her on another thread, The Cybil, Priestess of the Great Goddess and the tribes of Celtia. She too was struggling as her aspect; pain infused, fought a losing battle. Followers of the Old Ways slowly diminished and the Seer's Isle began to vanish more and more beyond the veil. Just as humankin must believe in their selves to lead a full existence, so too must they believe in the realms of beauty, the lands of the Fae or they would disappear.

In another thread in the silken web, something else was calling to her, a Littleshape whose presence she felt strongly right here in this precious and sacred place, yet unaware of her role. It was too soon to consider intervention before this one recognised another aspect linked them all.

Silver felt her proximity like a clean, sharp healing burst of energy and Vanessa stirred in her sleep. She was sharing the dreaming of a young Italian girl Nina, who puttered around an ancient but beautiful kitchen somewhere in a region unnamed. Nina, at first believed herself to be in the Italian Alpine village, where her dearest friend Magdalena was to have fled to become La Stregga but that was before the dreadful day her own mentor and worse, Nina's own father, betrayed her friend.

She remembered little of the apparent long journey and knew it was not possible for her to walk so far, even with the help of her fox-changer friend. Had she really, shapechanged too, she thought with excitement.

A stirring of the air caused her to spin around as the small entity known as Nangini appeared in front of her. Smiling at her recovered health and vitality, she scrutinised her so deeply Nina blushed at the intensity of her gaze. Nangini's smile merely broadened as she saw her young charges' uncertainty, despite her own manifesting powers. Magdalena had been strong but unable to see the importance of the link between the veil and her own gifts, whereas Nina apparently welcomed the power with a demure yet strong spirit; she would be a wise and potent force before much longer.

Nangini noticed the bag of Airmhid's herbs sat open on the table where Nina had obviously been studying; tuning into the source energy and the healing powers they held. Her notes proclaimed her interest and her shrewd ability to read the signatures of the plants correctly and Nangini was more than satisfied at this.

'Come child,' she said to Nina, 'there are things to share and show to you. Your sisterkin Magdalena has joined with her aspect Samantha and they are recovering together on Samantha's thread in the Skeins. We have work to do in preparing you for the task you face and to find the link that will help the spirit that shares space with you. While she sleeps within you, you will feel well and strong, but soon it will become important to find the other, closer to her in the thread that was her journey, for as she awakens she may take from your life force with her potency.'

'I don't understand fully what you tell me, but I have learned not to doubt the truth of your words or the need to aid the one who lives within me. I can feel her now; she stirs occasionally, but withdraws, apparently confused as to where she is or how she came to be there; fragmented.'

'Wise child, you are indeed, so come now and I will help you prepare for yet another journey through the threads that must eventually come to be.'

Jamie, fox-changer, sat in his canid form, patiently waiting for the next step of the journey to commence. He was unusually fond of the brave, slender woman-child known as Nina but knew as all foxy folks do that her destiny was one like no other. Her courage was what enthralled him. Despite her physical frailty, she carried knowledge within her for the healing of the blight that was sweeping the realms of the Between and that would manifest soon enough in the realms of humankin.

Vanessa woke, reaching for pen and paper, but they fell from her grasp as she drifted off into sleep again, the memory of the dream fading as dreams do.

Jamie still in his Fox shape pricked his ears, sniffing the air; something was coming. He could smell the Greenlord's familiar oakmoss and musk scent and something else; something that made his lips curl back in a snarl of hatred. He could smell *her, although* she was tracking Hercurin and the two Elf lords who travelled with him. One was Aithlin, his friend of many summer-moons and the other a young, arrogant elf who smelt of Aithlin and yet was of *her* making, by all accounts. Not so he thought in his fox-cunning way, there's illusion here; a glamour laid. 'Why would that be?' he said to the trees. Only the sighing wind replied.

Chapter 7
Aerandir

...As Above – So Below
...outer light – inner glow
...As Without – So Within
...All That Is - mirrored in your kin

Aerandir sat in apparent nonchalance, observing his mother Aelish stalking up and down; she avoided any trace of sunlight as it filtered through the trees in the clearing.

'Who was my mother?' he asked innocently, catching a glint of fear in Aelish's eyes before she turned her usual cold gaze on him.

'Why, what can you mean? I'm your mother, what nonsense is this?'

'Oh no nonsense, *mother*,' he replied, the stress on the word 'mother', clear, 'but does this mean you had sex with my Uncle Aithlin for me to look so like him?'

Barely stopping an almost animal snarl, Aelish snapped. 'Ah, it is nonsense indeed to think that I would sleep with my own brother and where did these stupid questions come from?'

'Well, mother,' Aerandir snapped back harshly, 'from the place that all questions come from, stupid or otherwise, the place where a need for answers lies, of course!' he exclaimed his cool, disdainful mask slipping for a moment in frustration. 'Perhaps then I should rephrase the question!'

'And?' questioned Aelish, impatiently.

'Who *was* my father then?' His question met with stunned silence before a glint of fear flashed again in Aelish's eyes.

'How many times will you ask me this? He is gone into the west Aerandir; he was gone before I birthed you.'

'Why do I have trouble believing this story? You look nothing like your brother, my Uncle, yet I look exactly like him only with your dark hair. Why, can you tell me? You shared parents who were fair Fae, where did you come to have your dark Fae blood?'

'Obviously somewhere in our lineage, there are mixes of dark and fair in any ancestry,' Aelish finished almost petulantly, before stalking away regally.

'Agh', exclaimed Aerandir, 'of course *mother!*'

He had promised Bethan he would ask, search for their obvious likeness that did not come from his assumed parentage. He was sure Aithlin was more than an Uncle to him, but perhaps even he was unaware of the fact of his relationship.

His mother, he was and always would be, wary of but he knew there were things, Magicks at play that even she could not hide and which he would not let go until he knew the truth of his parentage. He had no idea why he felt this way, he just did and he could relate to Bethan or should he say Arianwen, in her own search for a mother lost to her.

He sighed as he decided to visit Arianwen; he felt drawn to her. At first, it was simply because she was so beautiful, particularly for a half-breed but then her grandmother came forward, Circaea and yet another path opened for him to question his own birth. Circaea was Arianwen's *atara en' lle atara;* mother of her mother. He had heard the story many times about Minhiriath and the love

Aithlin had for a shapechanging water sprite, unusual for their time, mix-breeds being a strongly unadvised mating but which meant Arianwen was not human after all.

He closed his eyes for a moment before walking into the Between to find Aithlin instead. He found him seated on a recently fallen tree, playing a sombre air on his harp, reading the signs in nature and producing the sounds that would help heal and release the deva within, who was not ready to move on.

Aerandir paused, listening as his uncle played, tears welling. What's wrong with me he thought? I'm becoming as sensitive as a human girl is. Why is everything suddenly so overwhelming; he stumbled uncharacteristically, clumsy and Aithlin turned, a cautious smile of welcome on his face. Since his enforced solitary confinement, Aerandir was strangely aloof, not in his usual sneering manner, but in a way that indicated a deeper aspect emerging. He was surprised when Aerandir smiled with some warmth.

'*Aaye tinu nosse, amin irma quen.*' 'Hail mother's kin, I have desired to speak with you.' Aerandir spoke with unaccustomed, formal respect.

'*Aaye seler' nosse, quel' ta ele lle.*' 'Hail sister's kin, good it is to see you.' Aithlin replied, putting his harp aside and standing, took the young Elf lord's hands in a formal gesture of greeting, brushing cheek to cheek.

Aerandir coloured up at the physical contact; he was not used to this display, his mother always shunned contact with him. Strange and new emotions flooded him and he stepped back a little too fast, once more almost falling over. Aithlin merely grinned, holding him steady and guiding him to a seat on the fallen log.

'How can I help you, *seler' nosse*,' he asked.

'*Tinu nosse*, I am troubled. I have witnessed and heard strange things and I am no longer certain of my station in this land. I may be, *engwar 'ie corm*… erm, sick at heart.' He faltered before continuing, the words coming out in a sudden rush. 'Perhaps the Darkmaker affects me still, the blight follows me and I am,' Aerandir sought again for the word to describe something never felt before.

'*Gorga,*' he said finally in horror. '*Amin na Gorga.*' 'I am afraid.'

Aithlin, shocked, felt his heart sinking at his nephew's words. It could mean Aerandir would have to go into the West so as not to infect anyone else, for fear was the instrument of death in the Elven races.

As if he spoke the words aloud, Aerandir broke down. 'I'm not ready *tinu nosse*, not yet. I'm too young.'

Aithlin was speechless for once in his long life

'No,' a deep voice echoed through the forest; Hercurin appeared from the shadows. 'This cannot be youngling; there is a role you have yet to play here in this realm. Come, there is someone who can help you, but you must trust and not sneer at one who has skills beyond even your own elders.'

Aerandir and Aithlin were astonished at such direct words from the Forest Lord, but knew there was no other way than to do as he bid.

'Surely it would be easier just to tell me what that role is?' Aerandir snapped rudely in his fear. Aithlin and Hercurin merely exchanged glances. 'Some things never change.' Aerandir heard in the silence and grinned wryly in response.

Hercurin slipped with them through the Between to a cottage in the forest, hidden deep in the warp and weft of the silken Web of Tyme, where a slender human girl stood at the window. Her mentor and protector Nangini emerged, staff raised. Thousands of sprites gathered, thorn swords drawn, their stance defensive. At Hercurin's approach, they fell back, their chiming voices fell silent as they observed Aerandir's approach. Aerandir could not take his eyes off the girl. She was, he realised quite frail but something drew him; it was her eyes; deep brown pools of liquid pain.

Chapter 8
La Stregga: Nina 

A tiny bird alit on the windowsill of the cottage where Nina now lived. A small female wren with a brown and blue-feathered crown and tail preened herself before tapping her beak on the window pane.

Nina's world altered incomprehensibly and yet she was more at peace than ever before. Despite the trauma of loss and utter displacement, she was home and the little bird was her constant companion. She fed it crumbs of bread and seeds from her grain store, without a thought to her own predicament should she run out of food.

Her pain had not lessened, but somehow the distance between her father, Nona and her friend Magdalena's death, diminished. She knew she would never be the same and yet the wisdom beyond her years lay about her like a cloak, as if it had always been there.

Only recently, she tried to remember her mother's face; small and dark like herself; her father said they were two peas in a pod. Her mother had a tinkling laugh, like tiny bells and a strange way of tilting her head to one side as if she were listening for something no one else could pick up. Her father said she was a faery and they would laugh affectionately and hold hands. They seemed lost in each other and occasionally Nina would catch her mother with a small crease between her brows as she observed her husband and daughter in their closeness.

Eduard adored his child; why would that have caused her mother to frown, she often wondered but then, her mother was gone. Nina could not remember when. She had been a small child still; she did not remember a funeral; Nona spoke only in whispers and refused to answer Nina's questions about her Mama. What, Nina could not remember, was her Mama's name?

Perhaps, she thought, Nangini might know, or even Jamie the fox shifter who visited, who took her on short journeys through the veil to practise her shifting techniques. It was becoming stronger each time and, fascinated by the otherworldly gleam as she looked through the veil, she remembered it was exactly what she saw when she tried to recall her Mama's face or name.

Bringing herself out of her reverie, she thought if she let it go, then the memory would return, but every time she tried, it was as though the name had a weird schematic veil around it. It reminded her of a mirror edge creating refracted light prisms. Nina wondered in renewed earnest what had become of her Mama.

Feeling this was futile, she turned her thoughts back to her journeys and the practice she had to do; she loved where he took her; it seemed somehow so familiar. It was on the shore of a clear lake, where an otter observed her quietly and often water sprites played their complex games of diving and fetching, fiercely competitive. Sometimes, a strange little being would sit on a rock watching her. Jamie would always snarl and drive her away though.

An older woman dressed in blue robes would sometimes watch from a distance and Nangini too would come, to teach her more of the healing arts.

Nina occasionally saw the young woman, whose spirit merged as one with Magdalena. Samantha, she knew her name to be, was someone she hoped one day to know and to speak with; not just for her friend but because she had a presence that fascinated Nina. She could see her pain was deep, but her courage outweighed it all, although a small dark entity followed her and her little sprites battled to keep it at bay. She wondered why Samantha could not see it, when she could see so much else, around her, although at present Nina could see she was struggling with her shared experience with Magdalena and would, like herself, never be the same again.

Then again, a dark haired girl about her own age was beginning to manifest, seen only out the corner of her eye yet quite clearly. Nina did not know her or her role, but she liked the courage she sensed lived within this girl and vowed to find out more about her and her role in her own life. Could this girl be an aspect of herself, she wondered, as Samantha was to Magdalena?

With her thoughts continuing to drift, suddenly Nangini manifested at her side; agitated she indicated for Nina to remain inside as a tall, fair Fae, a dark haired Fae, the image of the former and her friend Jamie in fox shape, emerged from the forest. Sprites accompanying Nangini, were fiercely brandishing their thorn swords; Nangini, her staff raised in protection of Nina, went outside to meet the curious group approaching.

As Nina looked out, she met the violet eyes of the Dark Fae; his trauma and pain was so deep, she felt she would drown in his sorrow. Ignoring Nangini's instruction, she walked outside to face them and met for the first time the Forest Lord Hercurin; his beauty made her want to weep.

Chapter 9
Emergence

...I'm not all I seem
...let me into your dream
...and I'll show you the ways Between time
...but to follow me there; first come to my lair
...and trust me to answer a rhyme
...ask me all you will, I have consummate skill
...to travel all threads of Her song
...remember in truth, it is all by your will
...you learn which tone's right, which sings wrong
...as the way becomes thin
...come follow your kin
...as they tread the roadways Between
...for you're not all you seem... and if you enter my dream
...I'll teach you to shapechange your skin

Maeve, oblivious to any of the challenges her friends were experiencing, had no knowledge of her aspect, also known as Maeve. She still felt the grief for her little friend Alma and yet, excitement filled her at the triumph of claiming acceptance into the Clan of Scathach.

In her simpler, more innocent aspect, she was blatantly ecstatic; she knew almost immediately that she was pregnant after the Beltane rite. Her foxy-lad did not disappear, as she feared he would after their coupling. He continued on in the clan, wooing her, claiming her as his own.

He would occasionally disappear for a while. Maeve was sure his ancestry, causing the shifts and changes she saw, kept him from showing his gift to the clan. Maybe he feared they would reject him or worse; they were a superstitious bunch.

Maeve knew no different; she had always been more than a little open to otherworldly concepts than many; her parents claimed her as being a little 'other', on numerous occasions.

Only half a lunar cycle had passed, but she was convinced; she felt the first fluttering deep in her womb and stroking her belly as if the child already swelled there, smiled.

Deep in the Between Jamie sensed the child quicken in Maeve's womb. He was concerned for what he felt, albeit intangible as yet, he only recognised that something 'other' was indeed afoot. It was not something he expected to happen, fathering a kit to a human woman, until now he felt a little stirring of joy; maybe it would be more than one youngster. His strong, shaper ancestry would perhaps deliver Maeve of a whole litter of foxy lads and lasses.

He grinned at the thought before tracing his own scent Between to the house in a forest glade, where he sat and waited for; he knew not what, until Aithlin and the Forest Lord burst into the open.

Jamie snarled at the 'other' scent that came with them. Aerandir most despised of the Elven folk; Jamie refused to call him a lord until he behaved as such. There was no love lost between his kind and the Dark Fae who hunted shifters whenever they could. Why would his long-time friend Aithlin accompany his dark kin here, putting Nina at risk?

Hercurin however, stopped him in his tracks as he began to shift, about to launch himself at Aerandir.

'Stay back,' Hercurin barked sharply at Jamie in the Reynard tongue, causing Jamie to fall in a heap mid-change; no one refused the Forest Lord.

'Where is your charge the little Nina Grimaldi?' he said without further ado. 'I have the need to speak with her.'

'She's inside, Lord,' Jamie said. 'She's barely recovered from her journey; her sorrow for her friend and family is deep.'

'This can be helped,' the Forest Lord said, in a gentler tone. 'She must be woken now, and must invite me in.'

'...But surely not *him?*' Jamie queried harshly, 'this is a place of healing for the Lady Nina and the sacred space of the wood sprites.'

A rustling of leaves above, drew Aerandir's attention; looking up, he received an acorn directly on the nose.

Jamie could hardly hide his grin as a deluge of wet, shaken from the boughs followed, drenching the elf. He shook out his cloak with disdain, but Jamie could see he was not strong, something not right.

Hercurin looked up and the movement ceased abruptly, mischievous muffled giggles were heard; he smiled at their antics gently but shook his head, *'suula,'* he soothed and they were still.

Nina, drawn by the sounds of the sprites calling, emerged from the cottage in the glade of ancient trees. She halted when she saw the strange beings, Aerandir, Aithlin and Hercurin, although she sensed the latter's goodness, she was unsure as to the nature of the tall, dark male; she knew instinctively he was not human and yet not completely Fae.

'Child,' Nangini said, materialising beside her. 'This is the Greenlord Hercurin; he is our All Father and means you no harm.' Nangini walked to Hercurin, looking up at him from her diminutive height. 'I am honoured,' she said, joy rippled over her face as he touched her gently on the shoulder; she kissed his hands.

'Why I am equally so,' he said, 'I have heard much of the courage and skills of this young woman and we seek her aid for the elf Aerandir.'

Nangini almost hissed at his words; needle-sharp fangs appearing. 'Lord, there is much that needs to be done for him, but I'm not sure what you expect of her. Nina is young and untried.'

'She must call on those on the other threads who helped her friend Magdalena.'

'Will that not put her and who she carries, in grave danger?' Nangini said with unusual force.

'I see you have made an attachment to this little one,' he replied, overlooking her abruptness.

Nina came. 'Would you please not speak of me as if I were not here,' she said indignantly.

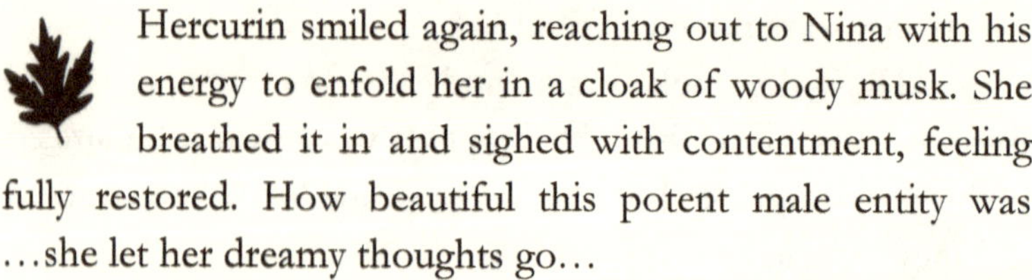

Hercurin smiled again, reaching out to Nina with his energy to enfold her in a cloak of woody musk. She breathed it in and sighed with contentment, feeling fully restored. How beautiful this potent male entity was …she let her dreamy thoughts go…

'What need do you have of me,' she asked. 'I am very new to this world. In fact, I would think I am dead and this,' she indicated to the natural beauty around her, 'the summer country Magdalena spoke of before she…,' Nina broke off as memory returned, her joy fading. Recovering fast she spoke directly to Hercurin. 'Where is she, will I see her again?'

'Not in the form you remember child, but yes, you will. You will find her greatly changed, but you will recognise her nonetheless.'

'Then I'm ready, for that shall keep me strong.'

Nina approached Aithlin shyly, looking wide-eyed at his height and unearthly beauty. He smiled gently and held out his hand, introducing himself with a graceful bow before turning to draw Aerandir forward.

Immediately Jamie shifted to fox form, Nangini raised her staff to point at his chest and the wood sprites rallied again, screeching now in harsh chattering tones at him.

'Suula,' Hercurin intoned again, 'this elf has need of healing and it is all beings due.' All fell silent but Jamie remained sitting in his Reynard form, lips curled back to show white, lethal teeth.

Unafraid, Nina took a step toward Aerandir, caught by the harsh beauty of his violet eyes so like his silver haired kin; his own hair, once dark and shining, now hung lank around a face become drawn with pain and wrath. She knew something ate at him, but also that a foreign energy invaded him, poisoning his already poisoned spirit. In her inner sight, she could see his skin covered in black, webbed lines, writhing with a life of their own.

Compassion welled in her eyes; Aerandir could not hold her gaze, lowering his and almost squirming at the gentle energy, she emitted.

For the first time he recognised the power of human love when it was unconditional... 'a rare gift indeed,' Hercurin spoke in his mind, then bowing again to Nina and Nangini, simply merged with the forest backdrop, leaving a sound of sweet music behind and the fragrance of oakmoss.

Aerandir broke away from Nina's subtle hold on his senses, shaking his head to clear it as if waking from a dream. He said to Aithlin. 'So will you remain here Uncle or am I to be left in this place. I certainly will not leave for I sensed already the barriers that hold this one,' he indicated to Nina, 'are beyond even your or my powers to remove.'

'Correct,' Aithlin replied, 'and yet it's not to bind but to protect and defend this gentle child on whom more than you can imagine depends.' With a nod to Aerandir and a bow to Nangini and Nina, he too was gone… they heard a haunting snatch of song…

…a greening globe, a shining sphere, that once knew only light… spun from orbit, falling deep, into the realms of night… once we knew the silken threads that held us strong and tight… were not to bind us, but to stretch, to help our souls' winged flight… and the forest fell silent as he passed, caught in his song. Fox changer Jamie approached Aerandir to sniff at his soft boots, whimpering at the smell of acrid death.

Chapter 10

Feathers and Flames 

...earth you are, from earth you came,
...your intellect from Air you gain,
...your Fire should burn, with flaming ire,
...yet Water has put out your fire

Bethan sat by Sam's bed watching her sleep, her little sprites clustered around her, were busy on her frail appearing form, soothing and working on new images that told Sam's story as they appeared on her skin. She was curious to see flames and feathers appearing among the leaf and blossom motif on Sam's bare arm, exposed by her thrashing around in troubled sleep, across her shoulders and chest and wondered at their meaning; flames she understood but feathers? Sam seemed to be oscillating between being there and disappearing into the Between at a rapid frequency and Beth was concerned that her psyche would be damaged by the trauma of her experiences.

It was clear that the rapid shifting between threads was speeding up and soon, Magdalena would be so strongly a part of Sam there would no longer be differentiation. This should by rights, bring Sam some ease of mind, as long as Magdalena was able to handle and disseminate all the information on the thread, including the energy of this technological age and its 'white noise', along with her own trauma of a violent death. They could only wait and see.

Hearing a sound behind her Beth turned to find Morgan standing in the doorway. He looked tired and drained; he was not sleeping well. At Beth's nod, he came in, looking down at Sam, an unreadable expression on his face.

'Did you see Beth?' he queried. 'Did you see Sam changed …she shapechanged to Raven? Why did Tara never mention the possibility that she's Ravenkin?'

'I can't answer that Mor, after all it was Flora, who received the feather in the first dreaming and Sam the leaves. By rights, Flora should be the changer with her mother's ancestry. There's something here that must simply play out, the more we think we know about what's happening the less we find we actually do.'

'Ha, that's for sure!' exclaimed Morgan, running his hands through his dark hair as if tearing at it would bring the answers he sought.

Beth stood, moving around the bed to stand next to him, rubbing his arm in sympathy as she saw not only the frustration they shared, but also his pain and for a moment, she saw a fine tracery of lines appear and disappear on his skin. Morgan felt her start of surprise, but let it go as she spoke.

'There's more here, isn't there Mor?' Beth quizzed him. 'You have different feelings for her than you did for Maeve, yes?'

'I do, but they are both valid, different yes, but valid in parallel threads. Maeve and I were always at each other's throats. I loved her as a sister as Bran, but Goddess, she tried my patience then just as she does now, which was thin in that aspect to begin with.

I can sense Bran was a serious and dedicated man and I honour the part of him that has always lived in me, the music too but he has a secret no one knows. In fact, I doubt he even admitted it to himself, except rarely, and it had to do with the Ravenkin who died to save him. She reminds me of someone and I question why she did what she did to warn me. Where does she fit in Beth?'

'Ah Mor, who could that be,' she answered somewhat ironically, finding herself thinking 'humans' in exasperation.

'Not you too Beth!' said Mor, 'You sounded just like Tara then.'

'I can't help it Mor, sometimes it's right in front of you and if I'm right, there's more that Tara knows than she's shared so far, but I'm not necessarily the one to tackle her about it; she'll assume Hercurin has slipped me a tip,' she grinned fondly at the thought.

'Well, I can see that's a possibility,' he grinned, his mood lightening.

They stood a moment longer watching Sam sleep, seeing her twitch and turn and the little sprites immediate response to her obvious pain as they licked, stroked and kissed her still tender skin. Slowly the blisters healed before their eyes, but then they noticed something striking, as she rolled over onto her back; a broad lightening streak of silver threads flashed across the front of her thick, dark hair.

Chapter 11
Between

KK KK KK

...as we believe, so it is true
...even shape is an illusion... knowledge hidden in you
...when you remember... when you awake
...who will you be... what is your true shape?

Sam only vaguely remembered, being carried through the Aethers to a soft scented pallet of oakmoss and leaves in what appeared to be a cave. A shapely silver-haired woman was dancing a circle, conjuring wards and bindings to hold a pile of ancient bones safe from any prying eyes; she wept as she danced, glancing up in surprise when she saw Sam floating just above the cairn of stones; the Cunningman Bran stood guard in the doorway. He met Sam's eyes with a warm smile of greeting. Although she did not recognise him in this form, he knew that something would jog her slumbering senses to undo the binding of her mind, placed upon her by ignorant parents in the thread where she now dwelled. A waft of musky perfume drifted on the night air.

Leah smiled at her and Bethan jolted back into her body, which carried them both. She smiled at the scene she had witnessed and vowed to speak with Tara. There would be no more prevaricating; Arianwen would demand the truth.

Sitting at her loom Beth drifted again into a light trance. More and more she was detached from the physical life as Bethan to merge with Leah in the Between where all truths lay.

Leah was tired of the games the shifters played, knowing they were a part of The Morrigan's crew of tricksters and that when these little Magicks were at play there were greater truths hidden beneath the surface. Now she remembered the day when Tara crashed through the veil unexpectedly, carrying the body of a mortally wounded sister. We must hide her, Tara screamed distractedly, all unlike the normally calm and often, comical shapechanger, Leah knew.

She gaped at the sight of the wounded bird-woman, caught in the change, an elf bolt imbedded deep in her breast, another in an arm that had almost shifted to a wing; too late to save her and yet she thought, 'but she's immortal; a little magick can't die!'

'No.' Tara said aloud, 'she can't die, but she must be hidden. Her body must burn, decay as a mortal's would, as it will when left without the animating spirit and somewhere in the Skeins, she must be hidden lest the one who did this find her. Much evil has been done and in turn, the one here, whose name I shall not speak, committed a forbidden and dreadful thing. I must hide her or the very web of this realm and all others of her kind will be forever lost and forgotten.'

Words came clearly to her as she felt Leah merge deeper still within her consciousness. 'Ah yes,' said Bethan, 'I remember now.'

Chapter 12
Maeve Hedinger

Maeve was recovering slowly from her grief, yet she missed the little girl who had become a sister to her. Alma's cheeky way reminded her she had not had a chance to be a child in that sense. Drawing the parallels of Alma being her aspect was poignantly evident, and had aided her in her own healing.

Content to be where she was in the Skeins, she no longer missed her 21st century life, having access to visit her friends whenever Tara would collect her. Slowly she brought a few of Maeve's less obvious tools and personal items through the veil so Maeve was as happy as she could be under the circumstances. Her friendships continued but she was not interested in a relationship, although she often thought about James, the journalist whom she met at the book launch at 'earthly rites', he seemed so familiar.

Her curiosity, piqued by his presence, she wondered where in the threads she might know him; she was convinced he knew but was waiting for her to remember. Occasionally a memory would surface of a young, happy woman; a seer who was wildly in love with a man whose face Maeve was yet to see.

It was a knowing in her belly, telling her he had been 'the one' somewhere on another thread, but she was content to wait and see how things unfolded. If there was one thing Maeve learned through all the ensuing events, it was patience.

Her health and humour restored, she was given the task of training the young folk in self-defence. The children ranged from about 7 to 12 summers and were mostly keen and agile; like all children of this age, they were eager to display their skills to her, particularly the older boys, who precociously ogled her breasts and long legs, loving to show off their prowess.

One boy, quieter than the others, would look at her with huge brown eyes. Ifor rarely spoke, but bore the obvious stance of an archer, already tall and broad chested for one so young. On occasion, she would catch him looking at her with a quizzical expression, as though he was trying to remember something; it was only when she caught him thus, would he present her with a dazzling smile …and so the days drifted by; post Beltane the air was sweet with the fragrance of wild flowers and honey scented elder.

Every so often, she wondered what she could do to help the others find Sybille but somehow, as much as she loved her, she had The Cybil, who filled that role for her whenever she needed a listening, unbiased ear. Her wisdom was so much simpler, albeit it no less exacting.

The Cybil would encourage Maeve to remember, to hang on to the memories of her 21st century life. Too soon, memories would fade and she would become confused as to her true place in the Skeins, her skills from that life, considered equal to those she was developing now. Another aspect would step forward soon enough to try her abilities, to realise the simple yet so complex truth, that all is one.

Shaking herself from her reverie, Maeve realised Pwyll stood observing her. She took to him warily, but often wondered what it would have been like to have a father like him, despite his disappearance when his children had needed him. Some things never change, she mused, considering the fact she had absolutely no idea who her own father had been, for neither had her mother. She was the product of a random act of coupling for the exchange of money to feed her mother's habit.

Pwyll read her well; so strong yet so fragile, he thought before simply offering Maeve his hand. He sent a surge of compassion coursing through Maeve and she smiled at him, transforming her face to one of fiery beauty. Pwyll took her rapidly with him through the veil; her laughter rang out at the rush of energy and motion, illumination and sound. They arrived in a heap of limbs and a grin, at Lily's, causing the others to laugh in turn at their antics.

Lily helped Maeve to her feet, hugging her in a shared moment of joy; she remembered her father's antics well from her precious moments in childhood before he went away.

Claire's eyes sparkled as she watched, thinking that they could have been her children rather than the stern dark haired women who birthed Morgan and Lily. Something else stirred within as she watched, a fleeting memory but she could not tie it down, something about their mother. What, did they really know about her, she thought?

Cal coughed into the sudden quiet. 'Soon we won't have to speak any more,' he chuckled with a trace of irony.

Chapter 13 
The Meet

...in each cell of your being... a memory lies
...it's not found in the Aethers... nor in deep blue skies
...when you remember... when you awake
...who are you truly... what form will you take?

Bethan received a probing scrutiny from Tara as they passed with Sam and Claire through the veil; Beth didn't lower her eyes, merely shrugged. 'So this is truly all about you and your kin,' she sent the words to Tara, mind to mind?' Tara for once lowered hers. Morgan, not far off, watched troubled as he recalled through Bran the scene he and Leah witnessed.

Lily greeted them all with a grin and hugs; a raised eyebrow for Morgan's tattooed skin. One by one, they arrived, Vanessa, Max, Flora, Cal, Alex and Susan through the painting's portal.

Maeve and Pwyll came through a little later in fits of laughter for some reason; Pwyll, collecting her on his way through, they sobered when they saw the serious faces of the others.

James, arriving on his own steam, they realised he had not been seen since the Samhain rite. Robert waited in the back of Greenman Ways, regarding them each thoughtfully as they made their appearance. He took Sam from Morgan in unspoken agreement, carrying her to a comfortable couch prepared in readiness.

Lily gasped when she saw the state Sam was in. 'She looks so frail!' she exclaimed. 'Is there anything we can do for her?'

'Tyme is the healer,' said Robert Cromlech enigmatically, 'with the help of a healing brew from the Goddess.' That said he drew a small flask from his pocket. Bethan recognised it as one similar to Hercurin's little bottle from which he administered Sam, when first she 'played' with the leaf sprites.

'Where did that come from Robert?' she asked him directly.

He smiled at her gently, 'A gift from the Goddess, my dear,' was all he would say as he dribbled a few drops between Sam's pale dry lips. She stirred, her tongue flicking out to catch the warm golden drops, opening her eyes briefly to smile at Robert before falling into a natural sleep. Colour returned to flush her cheeks with a healthy glow. They all sighed with relief at the transformation, turning to Robert with a question on their lips; he shrugged and smiled at them.

'There must be a little mystery left 'til the last,' he said.

With Sam finally sleeping peacefully, all traces of stress gone from her face and posture, the streak of silver stood out shockingly bright against her long dark hair. It had grown even more than before the traumatic event, strong and curling it was like a live thing, seeming to twist, threading itself around her. At times, it appeared as feathers and others as tendrils of a vine; on occasion, a spark of coloured flame flickered, lighting her face with rose and blue tones. In sleep, she returned to the cave and the cairn of stones, where a small creature sat with a pile of glittering loot.

I know where the bones are,' Sam cried; she thought she spoke aloud but there was no response. Her friends gathered in the meditation room to share their experiences and to sort out what to do now the Samhain Rite was incomplete. She did not have the strength to go find them. Just outside the window, a small Fox sat listening and waiting patiently.

Meanwhile the group assembled with plates of food, a mug of hot tea in hand; they toasted Sam's hopeful return to health while looking searchingly at each other. Something altered, changing the relationships to bring some together more strongly and driving others, as they observed rifts occurring, suspicion obvious toward Tara, from Beth, Morgan, Flora and Cal, further apart.

Vanessa may be the youngest in the group, but her courage was becoming legendary; she was more than ready to confront. Gone was the Goth girl image, they first met when she arrived with the group for a friend's birthday gift. Now her look was clean and simple, elegant even, in artfully draped clothes that fitted her slender, frame in subtle watery colours, most of Bethan's making. Many were gifts from her, outfits she had made and never worn or orders never collected. Vanessa loved her new look. She stopped dying her hair black; it took on the more subtle red-brown hints of Flora's abundant curls. All the others, having shared so much in the last year, were tired and frustrated at the lack of answers they knew Tara could provide, they still had not found a way to convince her to share what she knew.

Bethan was the quietest at the meet, listening carefully to everything each shared, but they could see the changes wrought by her blending with Leah. Arianwen lurked close to the surface; the two aspects combined, now became her, more readily. Bethan, once patient to a fault, was frankly over the games and manipulations and said so, her eyes on Tara the while. A part of her knew she had answers to much but was unable to find the words. It was as though the otherworldly-self had issues with what could be spoken of with humankin and what not. In this, she realised, lay the reason Tara could not speak of all she knew and particularly, not about what she had witnessed or where the body of her sisterkin lay.

Tara, reading her thoughts visibly slumped and then recovering, raised both her hands in submission at the onslaught of words from the team of ferociously courageous, humankin.

'Alright, already,' she yelled. 'Bethan can you explain, perhaps, why words fail us; words you most want to hear,' she finished, addressing the group as a whole.

'I'll try,' replied Beth, taking a breath. 'When I'm totally merged as my Trueshape Arianwen, especially since the last merge with Leah, I find the words seem to slip away the moment I begin to tell of what I know. It's almost like a bane that stops us; perhaps as Tara and Robert,' she glanced at him for aid, 'have both said before, we must find the truths for ourselves or the whole point of the exercise is lost.'

'*Exercise!*' The voice came unexpectedly from the doorway. '*You call this an* **exercise**!' Rage evident despite the cool, clear voice; Sam leaned, a little shaky against the door-post, her face set like ice. It may be Beth speaking the words, but it was Tara, she directed her anger at, in full, cold force.

 Morgan blinked as he saw the leaf sprites crowding round her, their thorn swords raised. Her hair lifted from her head, the brilliant streak flamed silver. She's magnificent, he thought, sensing The Morrigan close to her after her ordeal. He heard Bran in his mind.

'Steady Mor, steady.'

He took a sharp intake of air; Ruark called from the roof.

Tara and Bethan turned to Sam. 'You'll find out for yourself soon enough Sam,' said Tara, 'now that it appears you've come of age.'

'What do you mean?' Lily questioned, stepping in.

'Come on Sam, let's get you back to bed,' interjected Flora.

Sam gentled immediately. 'No Flo, I'm fine now,' she smiled; a smile meant to soothe both her and Lily, before continuing. 'I don't need anyone to tell me how I am, how I should behave or what to do anymore and that includes you Tara.'

Tara quickly smothered her grin and giggle of triumph as she moved toward Sam, stepping close to peer, birdlike into her eyes.

'Well,' she said; finally. 'I see that a lot has happened for you and truths discovered. They don't always sit comfortably or be easy to tell, are they Sam?'

Sam brushed the back of her hands across tired eyes still red from smoke and heat but shook Flora's hand off as she struggled to gather her thoughts again.

'It's true,' she said to the room, 'every time I have a semblance of truth, I can't seem to find it when I want to speak of it. I thought that was just me, but now I realise it's worse when it has anything to do with my own thoughts on the subject. When I'm detached, no personal agenda, it's just an observation, but when it's about what goes on inside, emotional things; I just clam up. Is that what you mean?' she turned to Beth.

'That's exactly what I mean Sam, which is why we need to find a degree of detachment, even when it's something close to us… or someone,' she trailed off; the group exchanged looks as understanding finally dawned.

'So that's the key', said Flora. 'But then how can we remain aloof from things that happen when we care about each other. How do we maintain that degree of detachment?'

'As in all things,' Vanessa spoke up, 'by not taking on responsibility for how anyone else responds to any given thing. It's not my responsibility for how my mother is, for instance. I can't change what made her that way. We all can only be responsible for our own thoughts and how they manifest our own truth and each truth is different based on how it filters; processed through the memory bank imagery we've developed. You know flight or fight stuff... sorry,' she trailed off a little embarrassed by her outburst.

'Wow, don't apologise Nessa,' said Flora. 'That's probably one of the sanest things I've heard around here in a while. You're right, of course; this is what Sybille always tried to teach us. 'Compassionate, yet dispassionate', being able to help someone or debate something without the veil of our own agendas creeping in to rule the process.'

'Well, it would seem we're making some progress, then,' said Robert with a searching look at Vanessa. 'Callum, you look tired lad, you have something to share?'

Flora reached over to brush Cal's sleeve in encouragement as he went on to describe the flashes of another thread in the weave as a young boy. Turning to Maeve, he said, 'I've seen you too Maeve.'

'Me?' Maeve questioned, 'how, when?' I don't recognise you Cal.'

I'm a young boy collecting firewood, I knew a little girl several years younger than me; her name was Alma but she died and sometimes I see you standing in a forest glade, you're teaching a group of us in combat. I'm holding a bow.

'Alma, you knew her,' Maeve said, her voice choked with emotion. 'Ah, I miss her still,' she trailed off wistfully.

'Well, this is something to look into,' said Morgan. Do you remember me as Bran, Cal?'

'I have glimpsed you on occasion and I have a sense I've listened to your stories as part of the training all Druid children undergo. Is there a way to bring these memories out, or for me to learn to merge with this aspect? I sense he may have something to do with my ability to far-see and if that's the case, then it would really help to find Sybille, wouldn't it?'

'I remember,' broke in Maeve excitedly, 'you're Ifor the young archer in training. You're brilliant and only about 11.'

Ignoring Maeve's comment Tara moved closer to peer at him, head on one side in her bird-like manner. 'Hmm,' she said, this is really getting interesting, especially as it was you who found our sisterkin's bones.'

Sam and Bethan exchanged quiet, thoughtful looks, but remained silent. Bethan nodded slightly to Sam in acknowledgement. 'Later,' Sam heard clearly in her head; Tara turned abruptly to look at Bethan, but she had already turned to Maeve, speaking to her of the boy Cal mentioned who could be his aspect. Flora, standing close by, heard a touch of near panic in Tara's voice; an expression of triumph was clear on Robert's face.

'What the…' her thoughts loud enough for her mother to hear.

Claire shook her head slightly, 'not yet,' Flora heard in the silence.

'Okay then,' said the ever-practical Flora, 'let's take a break, shall we? What about a walk, to blow the darkness away?

'It's zero degrees out there Flora,' said Max.

'Well put your hat and gloves on then!' Flora replied with a smirk.

Sam exchanged a smile, more like a grimace, with Vanessa and Morgan and strode from the room. Vanessa, with the excuse of finding her gloves, they had all come prepared through the veil for the cold, followed her.

Chapter 14
Tangled Weave

…twisted threads on the wheel
…make no sense as we deal
…with lives shared through the Skeins of Tyme
…for in one tangled knot
…we recall what's best forgot
…seeking only to find an answer to our Rhyme

Vanessa paused at the back of the shop, in front of the beautiful painting; Susan had created as their portal through the veil. She sympathised with Sam's outburst; her questions were no different to hers; what was the agenda of the shapechangers? Why would they not provide the details to help find Sybille? Since moving to Springsmeet to be a part of the amazing team who knew and loved Sybille Madison, Vanessa felt she had grown. Not just in stature but also in understanding her strengths, which had lain dormant until she reached what she called, her 'critical mass'.

She realised she did not like her mother and probably never had; there was no affection or true caring shown, despite her own efforts, although Vanessa knew not to expect from anyone, she merely wanted to understand what a mother daughter relationship *could* be like.

Now, with the truth out about her biological father, she was at a loss to understand why she was so different, to either of them. Bethan helped her grasp that Magick did not necessarily come through direct ancestry in the present thread, but rather travelled, quite haphazardly from other threads, even other species as she could attest, because they were simultaneous, rather than linear. She also made clear that whatever her mother had become in her use of magicks, corruption came through abuse of power but she would once have been innocent.

Dreams were gaining momentum and the dark haired girl she saw, about her own age, was seemingly frail and yet her will so strong. What was her real history Vanessa wondered; what secret was she carrying? She knew it was for her to unravel, but also that she did not have to do it alone, there was a whole group of clever and gifted people to consult …she called them her Magickal friends and her first question would be, 'Who was Nina's mother? Where else on the threads were Eduard and Max involved? Where did Flo and Sam really fit where Magdalena and Nina were concerned,' and so on, question upon question floating through her mind.

Suddenly she reeled with vertigo, visions of gaping holes in the tapestry rushed at her; she saw from a great height, the entire web torn and oozing in several places. One concerned the shapechanger Tara, another, her own mother, Annie, another Cal, another Bethan and her Fae father, no one was spared involvement in some way just as Beth predicted. She felt herself falling in slow motion, as she tried to keep it all fresh in her mind; arms caught her before she hit the ground as Sam, managing to swing her round to fall onto a couch rather than hitting the floor; her anger at Tara fuelling her strength.

Sam knelt at Vanessa's side; rubbing hands, become as cold as if thrust in ice water, while speaking her name repeatedly. Morgan, searching for Sam after her indignant outburst, found her kneeling next to Vanessa. He stopped abruptly as his sight blurred for a moment, seeing a shift in realms; being in one observing the other at the same time. He saw a small being falling into the dark and it was as though Sam fell too, he blinked and the vision cleared.

Vanessa moaned, opening her eyes, she saw the same thing Morgan witnessed and recoiled in horror from Sam's touch as the small dark entity became visible for a few moments; its pain and terror evident, she thought she would break apart with empathy.

'What is it?' Sam said urgently to Morgan and, 'What can you see, tell me?' with equal urgency to Vanessa.

'It's the Darkmaker, Sam. It's in… was in, your energy field… attached to you, but then I lost the vision.

'I saw it too,' Morgan said soberly, masking the feelings of dread rising from the pit of his stomach. He could not hate the poor twisted creature; its pain was such, it made him want to throw up.

Sam's eyes widened in terror. 'Get it out,' she cried as strange memories rose of a stone cairn and an ancient rite of binding. She broke down; Vanessa, recovering quickly held her while she sobbed. Touching her at that moment was the hardest thing Vanessa had ever done, wanting to recoil from a nameless something that was ancient and dark, of which, Sam had been a part.

Morgan watched, unable himself to find words or measurable emotions, for what he saw and felt right then. He closed his eyes as he let it be simply what it was, terror, for Sam, Sybille and the entire group of friends gathered. He promised he would keep an eye on the changers of the group, very carefully from now on and that included him.. He would never let changing shape be an uncontrolled thing.

Drawn by Sam's scream of fear, Beth and the other women rushed to the scene. Tara lingered at the door with

Robert and the other men, a strange expression, the closest anyone had ever seen to fear flitted; a dark shadow across her face.

'Alright, enough,' Cal said to something at the edge of his sight. He made a warding gesture; one he didn't know he knew, at something just beyond Sam and Vanessa. A shrill scream split the atmosphere in the room, followed by a childlike giggle.

'Alma,' Maeve called firmly. 'Come back here this instant!' For a moment a small wild-haired child, a smattering of freckles across a sweet, tip-tilted nose and an expression of innocent mischief on her open face, stood clearly visible to all. Her smile changed in an instant from sweet innocence to wicked malice; she morphed and shifted into the Merrow Mirdhaucha, but for a fleeting second before the change was complete, there came a small sob of grief and, 'Maeve, sisterkin, I'm lost to you, *look to the darkness in broken change…*'

'What!' exclaimed Cal. 'That's exactly what my father said when I found him…' He stopped, realising there had not been time to tell them about his experience in the greenhouse.

Flora took his hand. We both have something to tell you all but first let's take a moment here. We all heard it, she reached for Maeve's hand too. 'Are you okay love,' she said with her inimitable compassion.

'Yes, I'm okay,' replied Maeve, 'this happens more often than I can say; the poor little love she never really had a chance to live and Goddess knows what hell she lives in now.'

'It's all combined; all one and the same incident that's repeating in different ways, multiple threads and I have a feeling my role is larger than I can possibly want to know right now,' said Sam, then as an afterthought she looked at Maeve; 'and hell means a shallow grave.'

After a pause, no one commenting on Sam's last words, Vanessa spoke up.

'I agree, 'I have things to share about a repeating dream of Nina, a vast tree and Sybille is involved too.'

'Yes,' interjected Beth, 'I'm having visions again whenever I spin or weave, of a rite performed with Leah, a binding rite. I see you there Sam, but only fleetingly and you're drawn and haggard, floating outside your body observing us. For some reason I get the impression we're binding you. The Cybil is there in the background somewhere and Bran,' she turned to Morgan. 'You're Bran, helping the rite's potency. You're there Tara and you're freaking out about something.' She raised her eyebrows at Tara, not finishing what she knew but warning Tara that she did.

Tara's dark skin flushed an angry red, but she made no reply and the air became thick with a subtle menace. A sound of great wings, the wind rushing through flight quills filled the room as the Morrigan made her presence felt.

Cal spoke up finally, to tell of his father's death and the parallel of the morning's events, of the blight, he saw and the black webbing that held his father as he hung suspended, just as they had held the poor creatures that morning.

'I don't think for a moment my father died of shock or from a stroke. I believe he was poisoned by the touch of the blight and somehow, my mother was too. Could it be the more innocent a person's spirit, the more deadly the blight's effect?' he said, not really asking for an answer, the truth of his question resonating through the room, before he continued sharing.

He told them of his mother's sudden demise, from a picture of joy and health to having an almost unknown cancer of the blood, her death coming merely months after her diagnosis. 'The blight is linked to the Darkmaker,' he continued, glancing at Sam with concern, 'but I don't think it's the evil we seek, merely a result of it, a being somehow affected by it.'

He paused for thought a moment before continuing, squeezing Flo's hand and then turning to Maeve. 'Alma is another victim Maeve; she may have chosen her death when she saw you couldn't reach her, but the resulting entity, the Merrow, is not her choice but an outcome once again of how the blight works on a fragile psyche. Somewhere, Alma is still Alma.'

'Yes, I agree,' said Sam, 'there's always someone else around, unseen, a tangible presence everywhere the Merrow is.'

Bran stirred from his listening place within Morgan. He whispered, 'who is the one who has the most to lose, the one never mentioned or thought about who creeps through the hidden doorways of all your psyches?' Morgan could not find an answer but put what Bran said to the group.

All thought about it, but knew no answer.

'*...look to the darkness in broken change...*' echoed again faintly through the room.

'All right,' said Maeve, breaking the silence, 'I've gotta move my bones or I'll go stir crazy.'

'That's it!' said Sam and Beth in one voice, 'the bones, Tara! Someone moved them or Cal wouldn't have found them on the Wolds.'

'That's true,' said Cal, 'the marshlands hide much but where I found her, wasn't a formal grave and trauma fractures to some of the little bones in her feet were more likely from a fall than the pressure of the weight of earth found when something's been buried a long time.

'You took her body to hide it Tara,' said Claire. 'Where did you put our sister's bones?'

Pwyll stood, drawing himself to his not inconsiderable height. 'Yes, Tara,' he said softly, 'where? We all have a right to know now, I think.'

With a cry of despair, Tara vanished.

Chapter 15
Sybille's Teachings: Thoughts

...follow the pathway of your dreams
...create the scenarios in your mind
...what thoughts inhibit your success?
...what happens in the process to make you blind
...to the fact that success is yours within
...in your head, your heart... it's under your skin
...be aware... dare to dream as the calling is heard
...take a chance... spreads your wings and take flight
...be as free as a bird...

Thought is the creator of everything, whether it is a stray forgotten idea, a dream or a thought of anger or intolerance, love or hate... it's all the same in the Between and there is no judgement there. Yet, when we are unaware of a process we've instigated, somewhere long ago in the tangled threads of the weave, it can come back to bite us like a defensive snake.

Thoughts are the co-creator of our world. How we own or disavow our words, which become thoughts, to manifest as things or situations are, how our world will shape up. This said it's not to beat ourselves up every time we have a stray, nasty thought, but rather to be in the space where those nasty thoughts are no longer necessary as we grow to understand a different take on how the world operates.

In truth, we as humans can have everything we want, both to survive and to be in abundance of. There should be no lack or hunger, but as a species, we have not learned to trust that there will be enough and so attempt to make bargains with the Gods, who will play us for fools, if that is how we are behaving. Therefore, whatever you do my dears remember... where your mind goes energy flows!

Chapter 16
Stretching... body and mind

...a coracle drifts across waters deep
...to the Seer's Isle the land within sleep
...where the Otter swims free; on the shore stands the Deer
...and the Raven flies beyond all mortal fear...

They took the time to breathe, walking in the cold air up to the Tor and the misty edge of the Fae realms. Only hours in the Northern Hemisphere into Samhain and the veil was thin; a tangible stillness hung over everything and with it a sense of menace.

Samhain, three days of festivities that included Celtic New Year and throughout the three days it was best to leave the Unsidhe to their games, they walked in silence, each lost in their own thoughts of the day's events.

When they reached the top of Tor Hill, once again the village was stirring, smoke curled from hearths and mixed with remnants of the smouldering Bale fires. Newspapers, milk and other deliveries brought to doorstep and shopfront, rattled down streets as voices carried on the frosty air in morning greeting, dogs barked and the Rooks, siblings to the Raven, cawed a welcome to the sunrise.

An aware and ancient town, most of its inhabitants were more than bystanders to the rites of this Great Sabbat. A dark haired man visited each house on Samhain eve with a piece of glowing coal. This was to light their turnip or pumpkin-head lanterns to ward off any spirits who wandered too close to their doors.

Here trick or treat was not only for children playing dress-up; adult revellers would mask up to hide their identity, so the Lord of the Hunt would pass them by and the Unsidhe led away from the gatherings around the village, where the Bale fires burned and were tended all night. Everyone else would lock and ward their doors and not venture out past midnight after the dark haired man's visit. This was a festival whose roots, so deeply ingrained in the psyche of the town folk, it didn't matter your religious persuasion, the history of the district pervaded all things. Tourists flocked to witness a rite or to get, 'thoroughly spooked' by the solemnity of the energy.

Taking a breath in, Flora broke the silence; not quite knowing how to say it, she simply blurted out, 'I think I'm a wren.'

For a moment, everyone remained silent before all spoke at once. Pwyll stepped in quickly, 'Come on let her speak.'

Claire hugged her daughter excitedly. 'I knew it would happen Flo... oh and a clever little wren too, how appropriate. She can find hidden things in the grass or in hollows in trees... smart and quick...' she trailed off as from her pocket, Flora pulled a little tissue wrapped package. She opened it carefully, putting her back against the light breeze as she revealed two tiny blue-brown feathers, rust tipped with blood. She rubbed her head in memory of the moment, the spot still sore. Removing her beanie, she parted the hair on her crown to show the distinct puncture wounds where the feathers, ripped free, left their mark on tender scalp skin.

Sam visibly shuddered; not because of the pain a couple of plucked feathers would cause, but from the memory that rose to the surface. She repeated the words spoken earlier, which were unheard...

'*I know where the bones are!*' A raven croaked from the Tor and Ruark landed on Morgan's shoulder, eye height to Sam's face. Tara, appearing from nowhere, made a, '*sssssssssing*', sound to quieten her, why no one knew; Sam had not spoken aloud and Ruark made no noise.

Morgan and Sam exchanged looks of quiet understanding and Bran stirred in Morgan's mind. 'Ah, beloved lady,' he said, addressing Sam, 'you're safe,' before withdrawing again.

Through this silent exchange, everyone focused on Flora and her unexpected, near-change.

'Isn't this the time you say, '*Oh, I didn't want to be a wren I wanted an eagle,*'' quipped Lily. 'I know I did when I found out I was a blue-jay changer.' She grinned at the memory.

'That sounds like something Sybille taught us not to do,' Beth laughed, '*every creature has its own purpose and brings its own lessons,*' they all quoted in unison, sobering again at the thought of her.

'Come on,' said Max, 'I'm starving and we have to get back to complete Beltane in Oz soon. Let's find some breakfast.'

'No, wait,' said Lily quietly as she slipped something from her pocket, I found this a while ago on a gipsy stand at the market.' She turned to Pwyll to show him a simple silver bangle. 'Will this suit Flo Da?' she asked.

Pwyll took it carefully, running his hands over the shiny plain metal. He closed his eyes and small markings; tiny birdlike footprints showed on the surface, revealed by his touch. He smiled, handing it back to Lily. 'Yes love, this will do nicely for Flo.'

Lily turned to Flora; taking her hand, she slipped the bangle onto Flora's wrist; it fit, perfectly made for her and a note rang out as the metal touched her skin, sweet and low. Sam's leaf sprites manifested to take a closer look at Flora, their chiming voices drawn by her pure note in the melody of life, she understood, *'help us seek the other.'*

'Don't lose it Flo, always keep it safe.'

'Oh, I will, thank you Lily,' she grinned at everyone, pausing to wonder what the sprites meant. *'One like this,'* they chorused, indicating the bracelet. 'Yes,' she said quietly to them, yes of course. Meeting Sam's eyes, she thought she heard, *'I know where the bones are, perhaps the bracelet is there too.'*

She nodded briefly to Sam; to the others, she said, with hardly a pause between, 'now food!' Cheered by the prospect of simple hot food they trooped down the hill again.

Sam remained standing, Morgan behind her, Ruark still on his shoulder as they gazed out into the swirling mists below, where once lake and swamplands were. Drained for agriculture, the landscape was very different now to the archetypal memories that awoke as the two looked out over it. *'…look to the darkness in broken change,'* echoed in their heads,

Momentary flashes of light, showed the pathways of the Fae, who knew the ancient song and ley-line ways through the swamps. Ghost fires burned on the hills around to welcome the New Year and to honour the ancestors. A curious pattern of reflected light below and a series of images of a cairn of bones had Sam suddenly feeling weak again. She leaned back into Morgan's broad chest; memories began to emerge for both of them as they looked through the veil. Ruark nibbled on a strand of Sam's hair and the sprites came to life as Morgan lowered his head to rest against Sam's, their tattoos and hair merged, forming an image that the one watching drew back from as she muttered to herself in fear, close to madness…

'We're going to get through this Sam,' Morgan whispered. 'We're going to find Sybille, we're going to find your shape and we're going to be all the stronger for it. We're here for you, Bran and me as one; we're here for you Sam.'

Sam closed her eyes and let their strength be hers. They crooned to her, soothing her troubled mind…

Life is a mystery, a weaving, a spell, deep in the heart where enchantments dwell. Where dreams are ridden on brooms of light and butterflies flit in the depth of moon's light. Music is heard in the humming of bees and bluebirds chase fish in the sky of the seas. Flowers open as a new thread appears and all can sleep sweetly as she takes your dream-fears.'

They stood a while longer, determination coursing through their veins and with a sigh drew apart; they yelped as their entangled hair tugged hard at their scalps, the sprites giggled as they worked, disentangling it. Laughing, hand in hand Sam and Morgan made their way down the hill to find the others. The watcher's face, twisted with hatred and a sprites song turned to screams of terror as she caught it, turning it to dust.

Walkers on a guided tour of the hill shuddered as a cold wind blew through them; an Unsidhe passed through the veil.

Chapter 17

Annie Savage

...dark Magick... spell weaving
...how blind can we be?
...true Magick needs nothing
...that controls you or me
...illusions of grandeur
...to make one's truth clear
...is merely empty posturing
...that steals all we hold dear

On Beltane eve, Annie stood on the hill above Springsmeet, a space once sacred now profaned by the presence of the Dark Fae and the sad little fallen Maker, who fear held bound in a web of darkness. Her siblings, after attempting to free her, now held captive too; altered in terrible ways.

One by one Annie's coven members drifted away until only a few with darker intentions remained, caught by the Glamour Aelish laid upon Annie and, seeking it for themselves, became her sycophants. Now they stood heads together at the Altar on the Mount, reading from a beautiful leather bound tome; Sybille's missing Book of Shadows. Annie remembered the vicarious thrill of actually sneaking into Sybille's home, shortly after she went away on her sabbatical; Annie assumed in the UK, where she went into retreat to write her books.

She was not conscious why she did it, she was simply tired of being second best to the amazing Sybille, honoured and loved by so many. Annie had no idea what it took to achieve the kind of respect Sybille drew to her as simply as breathing. Annie's temperament was such that her inflated ego would not allow her to see the weaknesses in her own character; the very ones that now allowed the Dark Fae Aelish to manipulate her like a mindless puppet.

Words formed in Annie's head as she read the simple spell aloud, with the others…

There is more, so much more I can give you if you do my will tonight and again on Samhain eve, when it comes around on the Wheel. You will have all the power you wish for yourself and more if you do as I bid you.'

'I will,' replied Annie in her head to the voice that invaded her thoughts often, 'my Lady.'

The other women shifted in their focus as the energy passed through them like a cold shade, exchanging brief looks of surprise at the icy chill.

Annie drew their drifting thoughts back to the task of scrying, searching for Sybille Madison, gone now for so much longer than usual, with a sharp look of derision at their lack of concentration. 'Focus,' she hissed at them fiercely, 'we must find her.'

Only one woman, an old friend of Sybille's saw the truth of it; saw the battle raging in Annie when on occasion another face superimposed over Annie's suspiciously smooth, unlined skin. She remained in the Grove out of loyalty to Sybille to keep a wary eye on Annie Savage. As she focused to scry, the truth of it all hit her; Sybille and her niece Samantha were in crisis; Rose Dane crumpled unconscious to the ground, breaking the circle that collapsed, no more than tissue thin paper and where there is a void space something will always rush to fill it.

It was after all Beltane and mischievous sprites and Unsidhe folk were always willing to cause havoc with Wytches who flouted the law but deep within Annie, La Stregga stirred, throwing her energy out wide, she cleansed the cast circle with a strong ward.

As usual, Annie was not able to admit that this piece of Magick was not her own and took the congratulatory applause from her covensteaders with a smirk of superiority. Their respect for her strengthened again. Rose sat up fully conscious but saying nothing; a dark shape stood looking down at her, a beautiful Unsidhe female, a bow with arrow notched pointing at her.

'What did you see?' she hissed at Rose. 'Where is the Wytch Sybille?'

Holding eye contact Rose refused to look away; Sybille trained her true practitioners well, even if Rose did feel sick as the dark reached out to her with sticky black threads, torn from the weave of Tyme. She tried to speak, but words of denial would not form; her mouth dry, her hands became clammy with cold sweat. She feared she would drown in the violet eyes that pinned her to the ground, yet still Rose fought.

 A warm scented breeze blew unexpectedly through the grove; the forest lord appeared and breaking the hold of the Dark Fae, released Rose from her thrall.

The Fae retreated with a haughty glare at Hercurin. 'You'll not always be around to save the 'Onceborn'. One day you'll be elsewhere and I will have my way.'

It was as though the world stood still in the glade on the mount. Only Rose witnessed the interchange. With a respectful bow, the Horned God moved out of the circle and with a gesture restored the space to normal.

Rose, heard in her head, 'Stay as strong as you have shown yourself to be and she cannot harm you,' and he was gone.

Overawed by his presence, only seen on occasion in dreams, touched by his power and beauty, Rose stood up. Walking toward Annie, she said, 'Too far Annie; you've gone too far. You will upset the order of nature Herself at this rate. Wake up to yourself. Whatever's happened to you since Sybille went away, I can't say, but I won't be involved with your egotistical games any more. I'm all done here. A coven is of equals, not for some hierarchical, egotistical game play. Wake up to yourself,' and the group, stunned into silence watched her as she walked away through the circle of flimsy energy without flinching.

Annie Savage drew herself up to her full height and before she could stop the words that flowed from her mouth chanted, 'I banish you from this place. You are no longer one of us.' Her coven members gasped aloud and Rose simply kept on walking.

That's fine, Rose said to herself. I've thought about going back to the UK anyway. I'll look for Sybille there. I'm sure Robert will know where she is.

Chapter 18
The Meet Continues

...a new moon smiles in a darkening sky
...she chases wild spirits as the wind blows them by
...a remnant of new... an instant of light
...a moment of stillness in the gathering night
...a new cycle begins... new ideas taking shape
...she smiles on your ventures... from her fragile moon scape

They walked some more after breakfast, following the pilgrims, pagans and thrill seekers alike, down Tor Hill to the smooth dome of Chalice Hill and into the gardens where they paused to honour the Lady of Chalice Well, drawing just a little of the blood red waters each, to take home for their personal rites and for Litha. On then to Wearyall Hill and across the narrow ridge to look out into the Bristol Channel and on the other side, down into the deep channel of the River Brue. They paused a while, remembering their threads so tied to this region, while Maeve pointed out the places she could still recognise from her thread in the weave, where forests still existed right down to the lake's edge and wildlife was abundant on land and water.

Heading back to Windmill hill, they talked about the past as they walked to the part of the village that faced towards Wells, which overlooked the ancient ruins of the, much-discussed abbey. Its boundaries once usurped those of the Lady of the Seer's Isle and brought the end of the free exchange between human and Faefolk – the Fae disappeared beyond the veil and the Woad, deep into the forest to lick their wounds, as the folk were indoctrinated into the abbey and the way of the White Christ.

Bran, stirred within Morgan again, weeping at the deprivation of life and freedom his own people had known and the death of so many who rejected the yoke of Christianity. Familiar Greenman carvings lured the country people into the stone temples; lost were the natural ways of worship in nature, following the turn of the year and the changing cycles of sun and moon, Lord and Lady of the Crooked Path.

Returning to Greenman Ways, Morgan and Sam found Lily with a host of people waiting for her to open the doors. Colourfully dressed Pagan folk, darker dressed Wytches and Goths, clean looking Druid folk and the curiosity seekers all rubbed shoulders at her portal of vines.

One woman stood out from the others and for a fleeting minute, they took in the image of Sybille as she floated through the doorway, brushing past Rob, who smiled in greeting. Sam stopped short at the sight. Sybille looked healthy, so they assumed this was a previous visit of hers to Glastonbury.

'Who owns this building?' asked Sam.

'I do nowadays,' said Lily, 'why?'

Before Sam could reply Rob said, 'we did, Sybille and I. This was her other home where I could meet with her and we could plan when she would eventually move here full time, after you'd come into your own Sam and were ready for what awaited you. Then your parents disappeared and Sybille wouldn't leave you, although what happened now we couldn't ever have foreseen.'

'Goddess,' exclaimed Sam, 'is there anything else you might've considered letting me in on? Was I such a difficult person that she felt the need to hide stuff from me? I'm wondering if I ever really knew my aunt at all and how come we're all,' she indicated the group, 'picking up the pieces for something she obviously got in way over her head and beyond, come to that did you also know in advance my parents would disappear?' She broke off with a distinct curse.

Rob was silent, contemplating her words, ignoring the latter question with obvious discomfort. 'You're right Sam,' he said, 'we should have trusted you'd grow into your potential; thing is we didn't dream what that potential was fully, love.'

Bethan had a fleeting glimpse of her journey through the veil to the Grove, when she remembered the Samhain rite in Covenstead. It seemed to separate and spin round again to the present thread at Samhain in Glastonbury. She was back in the circle with Sybille but she remembered it was not Pwyll as High Priest but rather Robert. Seeing Sybille brought it back, and she understood why Tara had said Robert would be joining the Grove.

Something else to think about she thought. She also realised that now the vision fluctuated between here in Glastonbury and Covenstead. She went to speak, but at that moment, Maeve spoke to Sam. 'It sucks, doesn't it… the feeling of being a pawn in a game, I mean?' She hugged Sam fiercely. 'You can always come and join us at Scathach's Hearth and you Mor. The Lady Scathach doesn't judge us for our past only for our behaviour in the now and I say you've become the most amazing person I could ever hope to meet Sam.'

The others agreed, as they followed the nosy tourists inside and Sam's mood lightened a little. Too soon after the rite to be comfortable in her skin, but at least, there was a sense of purpose now, despite the pain suffered.

They all helped Lily for a while and Max decided to stay behind when they passed back to Covenstead and Wells. The Sam and Morgan, who passed back, were not at all the same people who passed through. They both decided to buy clothing they would not usually have worn. Loosely spun earthy tones interspersed with lace and leafy drapes; a feather here and there for Sam. Morgan chose russet and black, with unbleached cambric and linen shirt, soft boots of suede and a belt with pouches for herbs and little crystals, purchased from Lily.

They both let their tattoos show proudly on their skin the side of their face and brow matching like mirror images of leafy vines, feathers and flames; hair braided and held back with small leather thongs, hung with tiny silver leaves and ravens. They created a stir as they passed through the shop, unaware of their effect, on male and female alike. Not many could see the sprites riding high, clinging to their hair and clothing as they sang their chiming songs. It was not a statement for anyone else either; it was purely for them and the bond forged between them. Within Morgan, Bran stirred again and Magdalena woke up to look out through Sam's eyes, on a changed world.

This time Sam let Morgan take her through the veil as he changed and she could feel the urge to join the shift. Ruark's voice in her head told her, 'Ruuuark, sooon you flying beeee, aaaark.' For the first time in days, Sam laughed with joy.

Chapter 19

Alma

...she collects little gems that she hides in her wings
...she picks up a feather... to place in her hair
...as she gathers, she sings to all beautiful things
...choosing each little gift with such care
...combing the beaches for twigs and small shells
...admiring each piece... exceptionally fair
...hiding them safely in little nooks and dells
...for someone to find... if they dare...

Time meant nothing in the realms Between Tyme and to the little water Merrow once known as Alma, it was only a memory. She occasionally received flashes of herself as a human child held in soft but strong, feminine arms and knew that in her once human aspect she must have had a mother, parents perhaps.

It did not take much to distract her when there was so much fun to have in seeking out little gifts to give M'lady or to secrete away in little nooks and crannies to gloat over later. She was like a magpie, constantly collecting things that had no apparent value to their owners. They wouldn't leave them lying around if they did, she thought with a grin while snatching a small emerald ring from beside a sink in a public toilet in Glastonbury, just before the owner dashed back in to retrieve it. The young woman stood, a look of horror on her face, when she saw it had vanished. Her engagement ring; she cried and the Merrow stopped briefly, to feel her pain before disappearing into a drain, slipping back into the underground stream that would take her back to her favourite hideaway in the Chalice Well. Pain hurt her physically but it was always the most well received gift from M'lady.

Alma would occasionally take everything out to look at and try on, pinning a broach here or a feather there with equal pleasure. She tried several times to wear the beautiful snood Maeve made Bethan for her naming day, but it was uncomfortable and left her feeling irritated.

One day it snagged in her hair, tearing her scalp as she fought to remove it; a terrible feeling of despair came to her for a moment but she could not recognise the source. It sounded as though someone was wailing in grief and loss, but then she realised the sound came from her and she flung the hurt filled thing away as far as she could, giving in to the very human depths of sorrow. Maybe she should present this to M'lady as the ultimate gift.

She could not understand why the beautiful thing held so much pain and why the stones felt familiar, then she remembered giving some glassy shards to M'lady; having found them lying unwanted under a table, in the elder Stregga's room, where she lay unconscious.

Fear overcame her and she curled whimpering in the corner of her little hideaway; strange visions playing out in her head of a red haired human woman; what *was* her name; and a dark haired Cunningman of Magicks.

Suddenly she was standing in a strange space, a group of people stood around one woman, a changer perhaps and yet something was wrong if that were so, the energy made her want to bare her sharp little teeth at the danger the woman emitted. For an instant, she was a humankin child again. Alma her name had been and yes, there was the red-haired warrior she knew as her sisterkin. It was only a fleeting moment, but in her memory of loss for this sisterkin, she became lucid, '...

look to the darkness in broken change…' she whispered to her before the vision faded.

Somewhere in the threads she had to find them, to warn them but of what? Distracted again by a glittery thing, she picked up a finely wrought bracelet of silver, polishing it against her sleeve until it sang and shone with light.

Unearthly sounds rang out through the Aether …sounds of such beauty and richness, Sam stirred in her sleep, tears leaking from eyes dry from flaming heat, longing flooded her for something lost long ago.

Nina listened to the wind in the trees as the song carried to her; back in Wells, Morgan paced restlessly on a moonless night, when it ought to shine clear in the sky. He reached for his dulcimer to recapture the sounds; a new piece for 'Unearthly Sounds' but a piercing pain knifed through his temple where the sprites had worked their Magicks; his instrument fell from nerveless fingers.

Back at Wells, Morgan awoke frozen; he crawled off to bed, realising it had been a dream, for a clear moon rode high in a cloudless sky. Yet, in the corridors of his mind, a haunting sound, played out, disturbing and evocative, it reminded him of the sound when crystal bowls are played, rendering multiple melodic notes, at the same time.

Chapter 20

Bran

Bran sat in a rare, quiet moment, plucking absently at his journey harp. He was feeling restless, his aspect Morgan stirred within him, trying to reach him consciously but Bran was wary of the strange world he saw when he walked in Morgan's body and looked out through his eyes.

It was not only the noise of the mechanical carts roaring by; there was another sound. It caused a sharp, searing pain in his head and a rushing crackle in his ears; Morgan called it 'white noise' or 'static'. He would shake his head in irritation and withdraw rapidly, this meant Morgan would visit him more and they would share memory and information about the events they held in mutual interest, including their love of music. Morgan was comfortable with the more simple, if dangerous life of Bran's thread.

At first, it had been about Maeve and the small child Alma, taken by the water creatures. Bran shared with Morgan all he knew of the creature's origin and the time he collected the little girl Alma, bringing her to the Seers Isle and then later to the Hearth of Scathach, when she proven to be more than a handful for the peace loving priestesses of the Isle. Morgan and he were, through their interactions, discovering a new perspective on how the Skeins of Tyme worked.

One morning with dew fresh on the grass and birds singing a haunting spring melody of life, Bran listened intently as Morgan told him about Sybille's disappearance, the trauma to Sam, her friends and his involvement in the search for her. Bran agreed to help without agenda from his thread in the tapestry, carrying Morgan's consciousness within so that he might listen in when he went to visit The Cybil, for if anyone would know how to help, it would be her. Sometimes Morgan rode on Bran's shoulder in his raven shape.

Morgan told Bran, Maeve could be the one to help from his perspective. Now, as he sat, Bran contemplated the curious discussion he had been privy to, when he allowed Morgan to speak directly through his mind to The Cybil.

The Cybil listened intently to all Morgan said. She was aware of the disappearance of her own aspect Sybille and was at times unsure of what it could mean in the continuing threads. Silver had not visited for an age and this in itself was cause for great concern. It often left The Cybil feeling weak and unwell, something she was not used to.

She promised Morgan she would attempt to trance and walk the Between to find Sybille but was not sure if she was the one to do this.

'There is another,' she said, 'in a different thread, known also as Maeve,' she smiled archly at Morgan and Bran, knowing their connection to Maeve, 'brought to this thread by Tara, she is young and untried but is a promising seer and priestess to the Lady. Although it may stretch her, she'll have the strength to push through the veil. I believe they are perhaps aspects of each other, but not in the usual sense', she trailed off pensively. 'Sometimes through trauma or decisions made unwisely a split occurs in the Littleshape, causing them to fragment and this is what I sense may have happened to the Maeve aspect you know and the bright young girl of another thread, whose potential is vast, if untried.

'When can we do this,' Morgan spoke through Bran. 'Can we help perhaps? I know the one known as Leah through Bran. Her aspect Bethan is a close friend to Sybille …erm,' Morgan paused in discomfort, 'She, that is Bethan, Arianwen,' it came out in a rush; '…she's not human but a Greenwoman, a Fae.'

At that, The Cybil laughed aloud, 'Ah of course, Leah is an aspect of her and they are joined as one since Leah's initiation on the Crooked Path of the Lady. She will no doubt be able to help on many levels but I'm not sure that Maeve should meet her aspect in this way, the joining must come first in consciousness or they will change the weave of the tapestry itself.'

'Maeve has a need to know her life threads in order to make sense of her journey here, after all in this innocent aspect she has parents, which in itself would be a healing balm for her. Is there no way she can be a part of this?' questioned Morgan.

'It may put her in great danger,' replied The Cybil quietly. 'To come face to face with self is no simple thing, it puts two parts of one being in the same space in a physical realm, who have no knowledge of the other's personality or reason for being. It can potentially warp either threads they exist in or worse; cause them to lose their life threads all together, condemning them to live a half-life in the Between, losing touch with their Trueshaper.'

Morgan looked at her aghast, 'I didn't realise but of course this makes perfect sense when you tell it Lady.' He bowed slightly with respect for her wisdom.

'Now,' said The Cybil, 'we must arrange for a meet that can involve everyone who can lend power and energy to the search for Sybille, perhaps Litha, not so far away and will give you all the chance to work out what you will do for the rite.'

'I'll speak with the group, thank you Lady,' replied Morgan, his mind racing at the thought of the coming rite; how fast the wheel turned and yet concern hovered at the edge of his mind that the Samhain rite was incomplete.

'But it was,' The Cybil said with a knowing smile. 'Haven't you noticed the acceleration in the visions and dreams that, despite the rancour within the group on one level, is bringing cohesion of understanding, on another?'

'You must bring her here Morgan,' The Cybil said.

'Who?' questioned Morgan and Bran in unison.

'The one you call Samantha. There are the answers to many secrets held in this one young woman; not all will be happy with what she can reveal, but still, the truth will be told despite the changers will.'

Morgan said nothing, merely bowed again as he fought for understanding, then. 'So she had a place here too?' he asked, but The Cybil nodded and walked away, leaving both Morgan and Bran wondering who that could be.

Chapter 21
Richard McIntyre

...look deep within your own eyes
...masks off ...no more room for disguise
...what lives there, deep within
...not just under your skin
...who are you when you let go all lies?

As a child and throughout his life, Richard McIntyre's enormous appetite for learning new things, especially where the natural world was concerned, was legendary. He was a gentle child who dreamed of strange beings, who visited him in his half sleep or in the woods, where they told him haunting tales.

Like most gifted seers he grew up and in part, forgot the times when he would communicate with a beautiful creature who would change from woman to raven in an instant and who told of shape shifters and fae folk, goddesses and gods; in fact it was his own personal 'history of the worlds' lesson. She never elaborated on why she visited or why for that matter, she was instructing him thus but he was simply grateful to have his world made rich and enchanting. Richard never spoke of his strange visitor until, many years later; he told the girl who would become his wife

Jennifer was different to anyone he had met, in his parents' small circle of colleagues who presented their daughters to Richard in a steady stream; it was hard to get him away from his books except, on one occasion he heard a girl's voice in conversation with his mother. Looking over the balustrade into the hall below he saw a face he recognised as the only one he ever needed to 'see' and so their friendship began.

She believed in a world of Magick, populated by otherworld beings, her story telling later becoming her life's work and Richards's triggers for recalling his own childhood experiences.

Jennifer and Richard married relatively young and finished their studies to achieve their degrees in synchronicity, they travelled from the UK to Australia and back again, until they settled in the Yorkshire region where they both taught at the University, he anthropology and she, art history and mythology in art. They continued their writing, finally producing a work together, never published.

It was from this dynamic and amazing combination, Callum was born; a boy who had his father's love of knowledge and his mother's ability to delve into the myths of ancient days and write them as though they were alive and real as the everyday.

Years previously, as Callum grew and finished his first years of Uni, his parents would often disappear for days into the forests across Britain or occasionally wander off on digs with Callum, Jennifer taking with her, her ever-present sketchbook and charcoals.

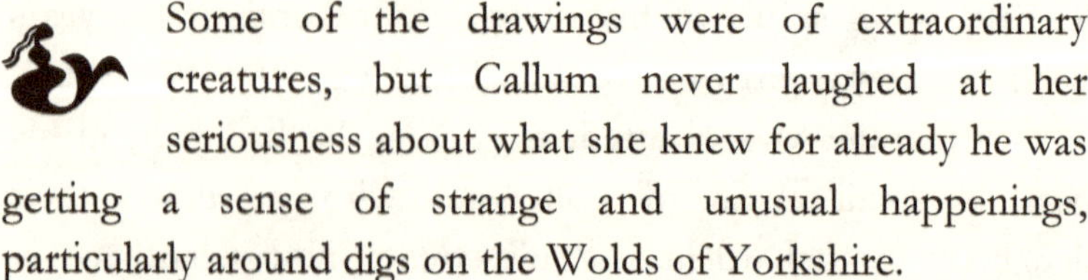

Some of the drawings were of extraordinary creatures, but Callum never laughed at her seriousness about what she knew for already he was getting a sense of strange and unusual happenings, particularly around digs on the Wolds of Yorkshire.

Unexpectedly, Jennifer discovered she was ill and everything went on hold. She refused radiation treatment for a rare form of cancer of the blood saying she would die with eyebrows and hair in place, *thank you very much* and not leave a toxic waste-dump of a body behind to be incinerated; she wished to be buried in the earth she loved and so it was.

Callum came to live and work in the UK to be closer to his dying mother. He found a place at York to study and make his intern ship and there he met Claire his professor and mentor, as he became a fully-fledged archaeologist with a healthy interest in anthropology just like his father. His parents and Claire were good friends and after the death of his mother, she was a true support to both he and his father as grief and shock overwhelmed them both.

It was for this reason he called Claire when, with his father in care and his mother into the ground, as she had wished, he found what he now knew to be, a shapechanger's remains.

Over three years later they were both gone. Claire remained the friend, mentor and surrogate parent to her friend's son, whom she loved and respected, particularly now her own daughter was in his heart and she in his.

Now, she stood with Cal and Flora in what was once Richard's study, looking through, all his and Jennifer's, paperwork. Cal had kept so much boxed up but now, with the permanent move to the farm with Flo, he finally began to go through some of the more obscure studies his parents had made. He was undecided about what to do with the house his parents loved, a rambling old croft, lovingly restored and a rare find, worth a fortune today.

Cal remembered the digs when they would visit him; Richard to fossick and Jen, draw. Claire told him as they worked, 'You'd be amazed at the things we've hidden from 'Onceborn', eyes Cal.'

'Could she change, Mum, I mean, could she shift? He asked Claire.

'Oh yes, she replied, but nothing you've seen before perhaps. You're only half-human yourself, Cal but keep looking and you'll find her and many other shapers you've never seen. She had the gift of far-sight you're now developing and could retrieve things from hidden places with her mind. There was nothing lost that Jen couldn't find.'

'Ah!' Cal replied with a broad grin. 'Okay!'

Flora smiled at him cheekily, the little Wren self-evident in her mannerisms more and more as she practiced the conscious change. She found it awkward and painful at first, unable to get her head around the illusion of changing from albeit a small person, to such a tiny bird. Her mother was a great help, as was Mor. They gave her a few lines of a rhyme to remember when she felt distracted by logics. *As we believe, so is it true... even shape is an illusion... knowledge hidden in you. When you remember... when you awake... who will you be... what is your true shape?* She would practise running this through her mind to help her stay focused and slowly it was beginning to work, even if she sometimes ended up with a few feathers left in interesting places when the change was not complete. 'Think bird', she would tell herself.

With Vanessa firmly ensconced, Flora grasped the freedom to take a little more time out, to travel with Cal and her mother to the UK to help with the clean out of Cal's parent's place. She loved the landscape and would comb the area for wild herbs for teas, medicines and culinary uses, bringing things home to identify, with the help of Magdalena's beautiful book. It was easy taking them through the veil to share with Samantha and Vanessa.

Now they stood together, overwhelmed by the task ahead as they looked at the huge library of rare books and boxes of stored papers and journals needing attention. Some Cal would keep for his own studies, others of a more esoteric nature Claire would have in safekeeping, the ancient history of the shapers was not for the 'Onceborn'.

Flora showed a particular interest in the sketches of Cal's beautiful mother, who reminded her a little of Bethan in some way; it was not how she looked but rather her otherworldly energy, potent and clean. Flicking through a rolled sketchpad of sepia drawings, she thought how Sam would love to see them. She turned to see Cal and her mother, heads together over a pile of anthropological journals and hesitated before asking if she could take them back through the veil; turning the page her audible gasp brought Claire and Cal to her side. They didn't need to ask what caused her sound of surprise when they saw the drawing that could be Sam to a T.

In this rendering the entity lay, back turned to the viewer. It… she, lay sprawled on the ground, but the elegant bones and thick, choppy black hair was all Sam, right down to the tattoos across the back and torso. From her shoulders one arm was human the other was caught in the change part raven feathered wing – part human arm. They could only stare at the image and at each other, speechless.

Cal, first to find his voice said, 'that's her, our bird-woman isn't it Claire.'

'Yes,' replied Claire in a choked voice, 'that's our sisterkin. I need to find Tara.'

'**NO**,' Flora cut in harshly, 'she hid the bones… why? I know the… the erm, 'Onceborn' mustn't know, but us? Can't she trust us to do the right thing? If Sybille is lost, could she not be in the same boat as the Ravenkin here, and if that's so why has Tara not told us everything? If this is Sam or Sam's mum perhaps…' she trailed off, unable to speak what she sensed.

'I think this is Sam's aspect,' said Cal quietly and there's something else I'm trying to remember, about my aspect Ifor. I need to speak with Bran and Maeve sometime soon. We need this done, finally. If we find the bones, we may find Sybille. If we find the bones we may discover who killed this changer and whether they had anything to do with Sybille's disappearance. Somehow it's all linked, but I'm having trouble getting it all together in my head.'

'We can't go near this with logic,' said Claire, 'and you're right, Tara has a hidden agenda that goes beyond the need to keep the bones hidden from 'Onceborn.''

'My thoughts on that are that Tara's trying to protect someone,' said Cal thoughtfully. 'I really don't believe she has any sinister agenda, rather more a duty to her and your kin, Claire.'

'I agree,' said Flora, 'but who is she trying to protect? Sam, Maeve, Morgan? Tara seems to have a lot of knowledge about many things, but never gives us the whole picture. Sometimes I feel as if we're being spoon fed only what she wants us to know, but who gave her the right, even though she's one of the Mother's Magicks as it would appear, so are most of us.'

'Well,' replied Cal, 'whether we're shifters or not, we're all the Mother's Magicks, just in a different form and I'm over the elitism of the shifters and the Fae frankly,' he continued. 'Firstly, though I know humanity is as children in comparison at times, we're all from the same source after all.'

He turned from what he was doing when no reply came. Claire and Flora were looking at him in stunned silence.

'Sometimes, you know,' said Claire, 'you simply amaze me Cal. You're the quietest of the entire group, but your insights are always, clearly and simply explained. We certainly do need a another session now that Sam's feeling better and would you please speak out Cal. Don't let your thoughts go unheard as you have a point that we all need to consider because yes, we are all part of the same source.'

'Shit, we're slow to learn though,' Flora added, so no wonder we're treated as the 'young' species.'

Grinning at each other they went back to their sorting, laying the drawing of the shaper caught mid-change to the side. Every now and again Cal's eyes drifted to it; it appeared to move and come alive in his peripheral vision. He knew this meant his mother was privy to so much he never knew about and yet he was the one to have found a shaper's body.

 Rowan, her name was Rowan; he thought he would find out what the name was in the Elven tongue; perhaps Beth would help with that. Cal didn't know why, only that it was important.

Chapter 22 

Rowan and Bran

...look deep within your own eyes
...masks off ...no more room for disguise
...what lives there, deep within
...not just under your skin
...who are you when you let go all lies?

A Dark Fae female stood watching the interaction between Brandubh the Cunningman and the shaper Rowan. Tension filled the air, palpable, sexual and forbidden; to date Bran resisted his feelings toward the beautiful Morrigan's child as she had her own, although she knew, deep within this humankin the shaping lay hidden; one day it would emerge.

They faced each other across the glade; they had never spoken and never consciously sought each other out; it just happened that way. In fact, Bran was more likely to see the Dark Fae as she stalked him rather than the beautiful shaper, whose smile lit up her face like a ray of sunlight.

Aelish's own smile faded as she watched the pair; how dare this shaper, this interloper make eyes at *her* Cunningman Brandubh? She watched him for years, never overtly approaching; she knew his reaction Dark Fae, as did all humankin, but he was no ordinary human, she thought since he was without guile. He did not know how to lie or hide anything and the concept fascinated her because all her long life she had lived by her wits, and used her ability to manipulate both others and matter to suit her own ends, ruthlessly.

Now she felt as close as any Dark Fae could to a human emotion; they called it love, but in her twisted Dark Fae mind, love was not about free will but rather in proving her irresistibility and using it to control her lover.

She preened at the thought, looking in the lake at her own image; of course, she was irresistible and if he did resist, well there were other ways of getting what she wanted after all.

Now, as she hid from them her rage grew watching. Bran and Rowan approach each other; Bran's eyes wide in the realisation that his feelings for this shaper were potent and forbidden. Trained to believe that no human could desire to mate with a changer, although he knew many who did, he held true to his vows.

At that moment, Morgan looked out through Bran's eyes in a dream forgotten, from years before any of the current thread events began; he had just made his first contact with Sybille in Australia. A few months into his training, she sent Tara for a first visit and accompanying her was a young changer from another thread, a child but he would recognise that child anywhere; Sam. So, the hypnotherapy worked, he thought as he woke completely. Sam had even forgotten changing as a child; her only memory was flying dreams.

He apologised to Bran, who at that moment had no knowledge of what was to come, as he fell, for the beautiful shaper Rowan.

'What the fuck,' Morgan screamed aloud, freaking Honey out as she lay across his feet; he soothed her, rubbing her ears briefly. 'What can I do? If I warn him, tell him about this aspect now, I can stop what happened. That would change history, everything would change but Rowan would be safe, Sybille would probably be safe and none of us would be who we are now. In fact, I might never have met the group or Sam.'

Tara manifested next to him with barely a rustle of feathers and lace; she looked haggard and drawn. 'Do you understand now Morgan? Do you understand why we can't intervene? We are privy to all this knowledge and powerless to change a thing; only the individual's free will changes anything, otherwise its blatant manipulation of another. On the thread you witnessed, was a potential that Bran and Rowan didn't grasp but he is a noble man, a Druid who'd never break his vows, unless to save her. Even then, he wouldn't live with the betrayal of his order, so either way as lovers, they were doomed,' she paused looking at him intently.

'Yes, I understand Tara, but you could at least have warned Bran of the potential and let him make those decisions for himself, for that is in truth, free will.'

With that, he stood and calling Honey, stalked back to the croft, wishing he could just remain here in the Wildlands of his border county. He didn't look back, wishing Sam were here with him now and that he didn't know what he knew; the knowing tasted bitter in his mouth.

'There's more Morgan, much more,' Tara called after him; he didn't turn and the door slammed in finality. He was done with the whole, sorry mess, but he didn't see Tara smile, she had broken the law herself in guiding him back to the dream but she knew the knowledge was in the right hands. Like Bran, Morgan was an honest and honourable man and now he could use his free will to choose the next possible and best, outcome.

Chapter 23
Ifor

...poppies, red, in constant motion
...nodding heads in quiet breeze.
...nothing judged there's no emotion,
...neither joy nor grief... nor cold to freeze
...being is a simple pleasure
...living now is all there is;
...be the poppy or the heather,
...you were simply born for this.

Ifor was a quiet boy, serious, mostly found deep in his own thoughts. He loved his training with his Tuath, his Hearth, as an archer, his broad chest, strong shoulders and fast growth in height, made him as big as most men, at barely eleven summers. His new teacher, Maeve was not of the Tuatha de, least not of any tribe, he knew and had appeared with the shaper Tara out of the Aethers.

He knew this because he had been watching the Lady Scathach, whom he adored, taking her Tuath through their training, when it happened. He had not seen another female warrior as tall as Lady Scathach before, although Maeve was slender in comparison to his Tuath's, well-muscled chief.

On the day, he was out collecting firewood for his family; he heard the sounds of stave on stave. Never able to resist an opportunity to watch warriors fight, he crept forward.

His nature was sweet tempered but he abhorred injustice; he would never let his peers bully those who were seemingly weaker physically and known to say, 'a weaker person didn't make them stupid; they may well beat you with their mind.' His peers; for both his strong body and quick mind, respected him.

With all that, he was a lad of nature, only killing when stomachs rumbled and only taking what the Tuath needed for basic survival, wasting nothing and honouring the process with an offering he would make of himself. A few drops of blood, a pretty river washed stone, even spittle, marked the place of a death honoured in order to live.

Soon, he would be old enough to go to the Hearth of the Cunningman for training in the arts of seeing, for not only was his vision keen but his inner sight was too. He could find things that went missing, possessing the gift since his first conscious thoughts as a small child.

One morning, he was walking back through the forest to home, a small brace of rabbit and a duck slung across his shoulder. He was weary and happy after an early start, hunting for the Lammas fest the next day. Autumn was making its presence felt, there was a fine misting of dew and crispness in the air that proclaimed an early season's change.

Taking a short cut through a particularly dense hedgerow of hawthorn and elder, he grabbed a few berries on the way to stave off the hunger pangs; with no time to break his fast but for a piece of bread on the way out at dawn. A strange silence fell, neither birdcall nor the rustling of a hedgehog or rabbit in the brush, eerily still; he felt a chill creep over him. It felt like walking through the veil, he thought shuddering and too close to the sacred grove at the edge of the lake for comfort.

He needed to alert the tribe. Something was wrong. Too late, he stumbled into the grove to see the changer Rowan, arrow notched, taking aim at a Dark Fae and by her stance, ready to let it fly. She was yelling at Brandubh the Cunningman to flee from the grove and he was attempting to control his horse, spooked by the Dark Fae's presence. Rowan the shaper grabbed the leading rein and Ifor saw her hoist Bran onto it as if he weighed no more than a sack of flour.

Other beings were stirring, stepping from the forest, tall and stately, blue woad spirals on their cheeks. Ifor could not just watch, he dropped his kill and drew an arrow, notching it effortlessly, surprised his hands were not shaking as he saw the Dark Fae woman aim at Rowan. It was the shaper she wanted, not Bran and she let fly two arrows at such a speed Ifor could barely see the movement.

What chance do I have, was his last thought as he watched in slow motion as the Ravenkin shifted and shifted again before she fell, an arrow in her chest, another in her arm, changed partially to a wing.

He stepped between the Fae and Bran, as Bran's horse bolted as the shaper screamed, *'Go, flee'.* Another Dark Fae moved out of the forest shadow into the open. *'Flee'*, Rowan yelled at Ifor, as his arrow flew to its target and the Dark Fae Aelish screamed in rage as it tore through her cheek; her wild arrow caught Ifor in the chest, throwing him backwards. He was dead before he hit the ground, his short, brilliant potential, snuffed out. In his inner sight, he saw the other Ravenkin gather to take Rowan's body between the veil, the Dark Fae took Aelish, screaming in rage and pain, with Ifor left behind, a lone spirit in the sacred grove by the lake.

He was a ghost, drifting, neither here nor there, his keen sight keener still and all his senses sharpened. A tall figure stepped from beyond, his nostrils flaring at the stench of blood. He leaned over the young lad's form, breathing life into him and feeding a dribble of ambrosia between lips caught in a death mask of pain.

Hercurin whispered to the lad, 'Ifor Callum, come back now, you're needed here, needed to carry the rest of the secret and keep the true sight to recall everything your friends will need. Ifor Callum, come back,' but he was gone and the Forest Lord wept; the ground where Ifor lay became a carpet of red poppies and other fragrant wild flowers that never faded, his blood ran free into the ground to colour the water in the Well of the Lady.

Leah came upon him there in the grove, carrying him with the help of the returned Ravenkin, home. She remained, as Priestess to the Tuath, washing his body herself and wrapping him in cloths dipped in sacred oils, before his parents buried him where he had fallen in the sacred grove. Richard and Jennifer, then known as Ryker and Jenna Callum-McIntyre wept but Jenna, from whom Ifor inherited the sight, knew that on another thread all would heal eventually. In honour of her boy's passing she sang, wings grew from her shoulders, small horns from her head and the grove filled with Makers and nature sprites.

Maeve Hedinger stood with the Tuath watching in horror as she realised whom the boy was and what a tragic waste of life. She cried for another lost child.

Among the throng of movement, a tiny bird sat on a branch, overlooking the sea of flowers and sang a trilling song of hope.

That year, the Lammas sacrifice was real, tragic and the Forest Lord honoured the rites with the gift of an abundant harvest for the Tuath.

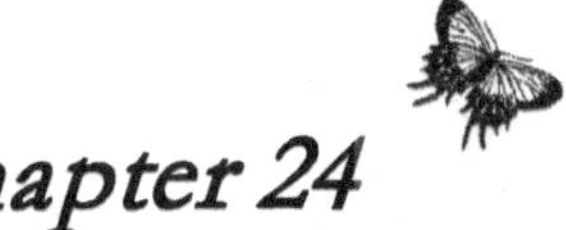

Chapter 24

Robert and Sybille ...earlier threads

...earth you are, from earth you came
...your intellect from air you gain
...your fire should burn, with flaming ire
...yet water has put out your fire

Sybille's notes to Sam

Earth: our physical body and our environment, it is classified as a feminine element, which contains all the others within its matter, 'Mata', the Mother. When we ignore the needs of the physical and focus only on mental, emotional and even spiritual self, we forget that manifestation for us, here on this plane of existence occurs within matter that is, if we wish to witness it, hold, smell, taste and hear it. We can attempt to manifest everything we need for our journey here using our mental imagery, our creative yearnings and our spiritual dreams of what we think life and being is. Nothing however, will manifest in fullness, without the ability to bring it into the physical, for that is what this earthly life and body is about, bringing spirit into matter, highest truths into manifest reality.

Sybille stood at the airport waiting for her friend Rose to collect her to drive to Glastonbury. She said she would be happy to hire a car and get there under her own steam but Rose insisted.

Rose and Sybille went way back; Rose once her student, became a trusted Coven member and a close friend. They met at every opportunity when Sybille travelled to the UK or Rose, born in the Isles, to Australia. Her daughter married an Aussie and Rose was Grandmother to a beautiful girl Nyla, so returned too, when she could. Who knew perhaps Nyla, younger than Samantha by only a couple of years, would meet and be friends one day.

Sybille often wondered what it would be like to have married, to have children and have lived a quasi 'normal' life but that was not in the cards for her. Her journey had been, of a very different nature to most. Her gifts; her abilities grew and her wisdom shone through in ways, noticed by the physical and Aetheric realms. Her ability to see had brought her trouble, on many occasions as a child. She saw her sister's girl Samantha, showing signs of possessing abilities that were more unusual, handed down through their ancient lineage. Sybille knew this would make things difficult for all involved.

Her sister, never understanding the Way, became involved with a man, married him and into his strange cult. The dogma prescribed anything unusual to be a sign that a person witnessing visions was either mad or possessed. That is, unless they were the cult leader, of course. Sybille had no control over the upbringing of Samantha but was concerned that the girl was becoming withdrawn and apathetic due to the 'treatments' her parents took her too. At least soon, Sam would be able to make decisions for herself, when she broke away and went to live on campus as she planned; Sybille only hoped it would not be too late, the damage done. What lay dormant in Sam was truly amazing, but how to tell the girl with Tara so resistant… well!

Samantha came to stay with her, when her parents went away on their travels to 'Holy sites'. Did they not realise that any land is Sacred, Sybille wondered. At first, Sam was reticent to speak to Sybille about her parents, loyal to a fault but Sybille could see she needed a listening ear and was shocked to hear of the control by the girls' father, over her every move; it was not healthy and it was easy to see Sam was brewing to rebel. Sybille made her aware she always had a place to come to at the farm in Covenstead and at least she came to the Sabbats and Esbats, if only as a way to escape from home for a weekend in the country.

Sybille loved to see her relax a little to wander the gardens with her sketchbook, drawing to her hearts' content; another thing her parents said was a waste of time. Now Sam was growing and had finally stood up to them. She said she was considering journalism, after her first year studying law, which was her father's idea for her future. Sam was bright, leaving school early, ahead of her class, to go to Uni but was changing course mid-stream, unable to comply any longer with her father's wishes.

Bringing her attention back to where she was, Sybille waved as she saw the car approach; not Rose at the wheel, but her dearest friend and more than friend, Robert, who she shared the business with, in Glastonbury. Ah, how they had met was another tale all together, when she was young and silly and did not know who or what Robert was and why he was unable to travel away from his homeland. She would like to show him Covenstead and the shop in Springsmeet; he would love the farm, the counterpart to his home in the countryside around Glastonbury. Her other home away from home as it turned out.

Pulling up, Robert was out of the car and she was in his bear hug, breathing his curious musky aroma again. Drawing back, the better to look him directly in the eye, she frowned at his serious face. 'What is it Robyn?' Her name for him and his Trueshaper name too. She smoothed his face with a caring hand, trying to read him, but he would not let her see what concerned him; taking her hands in his.

'I don't know how to tell you Sybille but the threads that are unravelling as we speak, are heading in a direction none could foresee; not even Tara it appears.' He paused, considering. 'Somewhere, and very soon, your sister and brother-in-law will be taken from this thread. Anne has forgotten her ancestry, preferring to behave as a 'Onceborn', like her husband. Their behaviour toward Sam has reached the point where their therapist's meddling has wiped all memory of who she is… what she is and if it continues her eventual awakening will change the course of history if she loses control.'

'What can we do Rob? She's almost eighteen, smart, gifted; can we not leave her to have a 'normal' life? Does she have to walk the path when she has no memory of it and what part of this has been her own will, somewhere in the threads, just to forget?

'That may well be Billy, but it's not for us to say or manipulate because we think it might be the best thing for her. Only she knows that in truth.'

'But… what about you Rob? Can't you do something?'

'If I were to show my hand, I would be up against The Morrigan and all her clan. They want her back in the fold and I can understand that because without her, the Lady Herself has a void space and we know what happens with a void don't we; we've seen it through history often enough. We can't let the possible outcome affect the earth plane. If we do, we are forgetting out part. We are caretakers of the planet, not for those humankin who are more aware, but for the innocents, the 'Onceborn', those lost and confused, enough, without finding out that all their beliefs are nothing if the Shining Ones are lost. One day they will wake up to the fact that they are all a part of the greater whole, all part of Her Magicks.'

He sighed, hefting Sybille's bags into the back of the car and opening the door for her, like the gentleman, he was. 'But this is no way to greet my dearest friend,' he said, grinning ruefully. 'Welcome home my love, it's been too long and the house is empty without you. When will you come for good,' he said, 'retire and live here in harmony and comfort with me?'

'Ah, well,' she said, 'that brings us full circle to where we started this conversation… Samantha. I can't, at least not until she knows what her role is, what her ancestry is and that she is strong and free to live as she pleases.'

'All these things she must find for herself,' said Rob.

'Yes I know, but if her parents are to be taken away, she will have only me and I want to be there if possible when her change comes.'

'Yes, fair enough.' Robert sighed again. 'It will be as it will be. Enough now tell me what's been going on for you at work and home. How are all your students shaping up this year?'

'All fairly straightforward this season, none who stand out.'

'You won't be saying that in a couple of years when the Grove forms Billy,' Rob grinned. 'They'll keep you on your toes.'

'Will I know them; recognise them straight away do you think?'

'Oh yes, I'm sure you will and not just from this thread my love but from many. Now I thought we'd stop for a bite to eat on the way back?'

'Lovely, I'm starving.' Sybille settled back in her seat, feeling a little woozy and already jet-lagged; Rob let her be.

Then she was flying above the ground high over mountaintops; her friend Tara and a host of the Ravenkin were flying too. Her sister was the first to spot the huge flock, pointing them out to her husband.

'Godless lot ravens,' he said, disgruntled with the heat and flies; just wanting to get to the caves their guide was taking them too, where artefacts had been found that were said to be linked to the origins of his cult.

Sybille knew she was dreaming, but could not rouse herself, helpless, she witnessed her sister and husband taken from a site high in a mountain range in the Middle East, lifted from the ground by the Ravenkin, their guide fell on his knees, covering his head with his hands. Who would believe this, he thought and then the flock and the two difficult English people simply disappeared. It was as though a hole appeared into nowhere and they were gone. Sybille wondered quite lucidly if she would ever see them again. One day she would remember those thoughts when they came back to haunt her.

She jerked awake as she hit her physical body hard on re-entry, shaken and teary. 'It's happened Rob. They're gone. I'm going to need to go back early so that I'm at least in the country, when Sam hears. Why couldn't Tara have warned me… ugh no, don't answer that. No one is to interfere, although it seems to me that this is exactly that, interference.

'It may take a few days for anyone to realise they're even missing,' said Rob quietly, ignoring her natural need to vent.

'Well they were supposed to call me tonight to organise Sam's eighteenth coming up; they weren't sure they'd be back for it and if they don't ring, I'm going to be the one to report them missing aren't I?'

'Well, better that way Billy,' at least you know they'll be alright and be better equipped to help Sam through this.'

'That's true, but it doesn't make it any easier. Will we see them again on this thread do you think? Poor Sam, she'll be caught in a difficult situation, free to do as she wants and feeling guilty if she's happy at the thought. We were never close, my sister and I but she's my only kin, other than Sam and now, it's done and I have to go through the whole rigmarole of planning a funeral that is a farce. I think you need to take me back to the airport Rob. She saw his face fall, but he recovered himself quickly, as always, the one to do what was necessary in such a crisis.

'Talk about a flying visit,' he grinned, but there was pain in his eyes.

Chapter 25

Billy and Tats

Lammas two years ago

...deep within the Wylde dreamer stirs
...awakening from slumber as change occurs
...be willing to sense how your own needs are met
...stay awake, be aware... lest your dreams you forget
...you are the sleeper and you are the dream
...one and the same... it's within to be seen
... you have slept long enough, wake up human kin
...awaken Wylde dreamer... let the magicks begin

Tara sat with Sybille on the back verandah at Covenstead, shaded by the ancient elders. It was close to Lammas and Indian summer set in, after a wild wet month. Elderflower petals still lay on the ground like fragrant powdered snow as the nubbly berries began to sprout in green umbels... within a week they would fill with juice and begin their burgundy colour change.

They sat in companionable silence, watching the antics of the nature sprites and the marauding shapers who came and went everywhere Tara did. The sun was beginning to set and far away as in a dream, they could hear the sound of Hercurin's pipe. Sweet yet sorrowful, as the end of his time among them diminished... soon he would be the shadow that lived in the forests, sacrificing his life for the grain harvest, to lie down again at the feet of the Lady.

Sybille sighed, 'all right Tats spit it out, what's going on with you?'

Tara hesitated, there was very little she did not tell her friend yet, she had difficulty with this particular subject. Taking a sharp breath in she took a sip of her hot chocolate, considering what and how much she could tell Sybille, before beginning. 'It's gone, Billy, her body's gone.'

'Whose body... ah, you mean your sisterkin. You hid her; why I don't know, but I do know at some stage, Samantha could be involved with her. When are you going to tell me Tats?' You see so much more of the weave of the Lady's threads. I'll be going in a couple of months to renew and you know I told you the other day I was feeling as if it would be sooner than usual. Please don't let me leave again without preparing Sam for it, as you know I have been having strange dreams and it involves all my girls to some degree. I've left things for them to read and hope against hope it will all be as usual but something tells me all is not well in the Between.'

'Ah, Billy I wish I could, but you know how it is when the threads become entangled. Sometimes I think our meddling makes it worse, but still we do what we must. I don't want to play with people's lives, but the Mother is moving things towards an outcome I can't fathom and yes, all the girls will be involved, but it's simply because it's time they woke up... we need more people to wake up. So many are becoming aware of the Old Ways, the Crooked Path and yet they're not 'real'. For most it's more about the image than the truth of what it means to be a Wytch as a way of life, not just something we do when the sun or moon are in a particular position or wearing the right clothes while chanting spells.'

'Where is this going Tats,' Sybille interrupted her meanderings. 'Are you going to tell me what's going on or not?' Before Tara could reply, everything began to move and shift in Sybille's vision.

'Are you okay, Billy,' Tara asked her, although she could clearly see that the shift to renewal was close.

'Err, yes, I'll be fine, but I should go finish getting ready… it's very close Tats.'

Tara hugged her friend and left wordlessly. After all, there was nothing to say and the Mother would have her way. She changed as she was leaving, lifting off in a cloud of musk, lace and feathers.

Sybille went to her desk, where Morgana lay sprawled across her journal, to finish the notes to her students before putting them in a package with a wad of documents. Arranging so many things in the event of her leaving early, she hoped nothing was forgotten.

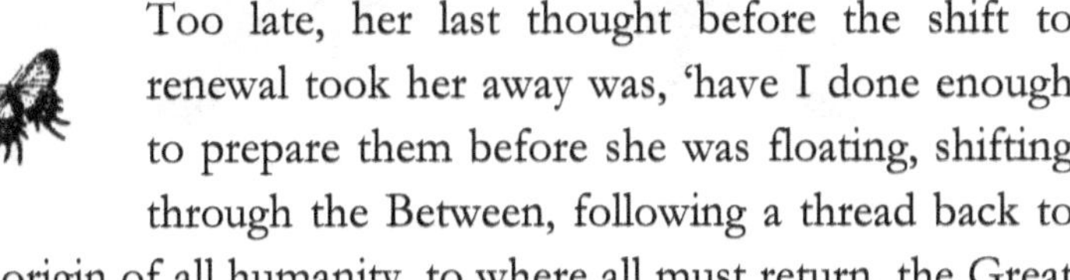

Too late, her last thought before the shift to renewal took her away was, 'have I done enough to prepare them before she was floating, shifting through the Between, following a thread back to the origin of all humanity, to where all must return, the Great Birthing Tree, where Silver waited.

Chapter 26

Cal and Flora

...night drifts into day... there's so much in play
...as the planet spins on through space
...we take it as given it will always be here
...but have you truly found your place
...as the stars spin away... and night drifts into day
...can you say you have done all you can
...is the world better for you... have you lived life with grace
...or do you sense this is the downfall of man
...have we all done our best... have we worked without rest?
...to fulfil the dreams of a greening life
...when we came here to play... did we dream of this day
...as the planet is torn by war and strife
...so if you feel there's more to do... don't speak of 'they', make it 'you'
...who travels the earth path with joy, not fear
...then who knows, if we're strong... we will finally right the wrong
...to renew the world and dry each child's tear

Flora, shocked awake by Cal's scream of pain, fumbled for the light by the bed. Split seconds later, with a thunder of feet up the stairs and from across the hall, the door flew open as Vanessa and Samantha hurtled into the room, woken by Cal's cry and through the pure instinct formed, by the closely meshed group.

Flora knelt by Cal on the bed trying to wake him. He was soaked and at first, she thought it was excessive sweat from the dream, but as she drew her hand out from under the cover, she almost passed out; it was blood, warm and pumping and she simply froze.

Throwing back the covers without thought for Cal's dignity, Samantha grabbed the sheet and went to work instinctively, putting pressure on the wound while avoiding the blue-feather tipped shaft that was embedded deep in the sternum, calling the while silently, for help. First aid was one thing this was something else and they could not even call for an ambulance.

Claire hearing her daughter's cry in her head, changed, flew down to the house and changing again, ran up the stairs. What she saw shocked her to the core. Cal lay covered in blood, still seeping from an obvious arrow wound in his chest. She sent a prayer and a cry for help out into the Aether and the response was immediate. She gave permission in her head for their entry into the house. From seemingly, out of nowhere a host of owl and raven changers were there, carrying Cal away.

Tara turned to Sam briefly as she left; taking in the shocked faces of the four women and seeing Flora going into shock, she produced a small vial of amber liquid. 'This is for the shock, you all need to take it and Sam,' Sam looked at Tara, her eyes seething with anger. 'That's right Sam, get angry. It's okay to get angry with this completely sorry mess. Then get angrier and remember your part in the creation of it. Your parents in this thread wiped you clean, but the cells of memory are still in you and operative.'

With that said, she followed her kin, who were taking Cal away, calling over her shoulder to Flora, 'He'll be alright Flo, this is a cell memory gone berserk and can be healed with the right help. Call on your clan Flo,' and was gone.

They looked at each other numbly; Vanessa went to work to clear away the bloodstained sheets; taking them away, Clair drew Flora downstairs.

'Come on Flo,' said Sam gently handing the small vial to Claire. 'Take the drops and some tea; the Ravenkin will help him. I…' she wiped her hand across the back of her face almost savagely as tears fell and before anyone had time to react, Sam changed, her change fuelled by such anger, it happened completely and fast.

She flew in Raven form around the room, seeking a physical way out, her sprites assembling around her in victory. Claire managed to open the window as Sam merged with Ruark for the first time.

Down below a car door slammed and Claire saw Morgan and Beth get out the car; Morgan saw the Raven shape and knew. Changing rapidly he flew, calling on the Morrigan for help as Sam took flight.

Morgan could barely keep up with her, but could hear her thoughts seething with anger and outrage.

'Cal! *No*, not Cal,' he heard shocked almost into change back to human form mid-flight. 'He's the most beautiful, clean soul; Flo adores him; *no, not Cal.*'

What had happened to Cal he thought, but continued to follow Sam; he could not let her make this journey alone in the state she was in, no matter what the cause. Bran rose to the surface, showing him the images again of the moments captured in his cells, when the Ravenshaper Rowan saved his life. What was not seen before was the boy Ifor, standing between to make his mark on the Dark Fae Aelish and to take the arrow that ended his short, promising life.

Merged as one they flew together, following Sam through the Aethers, through the veil and deep into the Between. Magdalena stirred within Sam, concerned, as Rowan too became one with them.

Morgan could see the occasional blue-orange flame lick across her inky-black wings and began to understand.

Earth you are, from earth you came, your intellect from Air you gain, your Fire should burn, with flaming ire yet Water has put out your fire... Sam's earthy nature and the leaf sprites who reminded her of her journey, were the catalyst for her to ground herself physically, the emotions of her life with her parents when they had 'doused' all her fire with their own needs to control, were finally breaking her free of anyone's influence. Even under the circumstances, if a Raven could grin, Morgan did.

Tara and the Ravenkin took Cal's failing body to the place where Ifor had died. Laying him in the bed of wild flowers, and calling for their Trueshape, 'The Morrigan', to help them. She didn't appear. Tara knew that without Cal, there was a void space again in the web that no one could fill. He would never have found the body of her sister, never have met Flora and never been there to save his father from being dragged into the void. He would never have drawn breath as Callum McIntyre and the Skeins of Tyme would never be the same. Cal would be no more than a possibility.

Jamie sat in his fox shape. Going against all instructions to keep Nina safe, her presence hidden and unknown to the Dark Fae, he approached the still body of Cal, whom he liked enormously from the thread he shared with him and the extraordinary group of courageous humankin.

Hailing Tara and Claire in their bird forms, Jamie made a suggestion that could alter everything. He whispered to them of his charge the young La Stregga Nina, hidden on an altered thread in the forest on the lakeshore, not far away in the physical realm.

Claire took a deep breath, looking at Tara. 'Did you know this?' she said in the birdkin tongue'

Tara shook her head. 'No, there are things even we are not privy of.'

'Then let's go,' said Claire changing form to help carry Cal physically, as Jamie led them through a glowing veil of protection into a quiet clearing, near a small cottage.

Nangini, not easily swayed, stood with the sprites to protect and defend Nina and the secret cargo the girl carried but once again, Nina could not allow anyone to suffer as she saw the body they carried.

'Bring him inside,' she demanded, fire and water sprites hastened to stir the fire in the hearth and bring water to boil, unbidden.

A little wren landed on the window ledge, tapping frantically on the glass. Nina moved quickly letting the little bird in as with a flutter of tiny wings she entered and changed, rushing to the bed where they'd laid Cal's still form.

Frozen to the chair in the corner, the Elf Lord Aerandir sat; he had nowhere to go. Spotting him there, the entire crew turned as one; in the mood they were in, they could tear him to shreds and hang the consequences.

Jamie stopped them with his yell. 'No,' he cried, 'he is here under Hercurin's protection for healing, or else he will be sent into the West and the Forest Lord has spoken that it's too soon for this young Fae… he was not born Dark and it's this that we also have to help him sort out. In fact, he claims… he believes… Aelish is not his mother at all.' It all came out in a rush as the group took it all in.

Flora and Nina were at the bedside, not caring what else was going on; both feared for the man. The sheet, now dried with Cal's blood, adhered around the wound. They removed it, moistening with soft clean cloths, soaked in warm water and a solution of All-heal in alcohol, to prevent infection.

Spotting the Bag of Airmhid on the table, Flora automatically went to find what she could to help Cal, while they dealt with extracting the arrowhead.

Tara, using her sharp beak, snipped off the arrow shaft the better to get to the wound. Cal groaned, but did not wake up. Nangini stepped forward quickly to prevent Flora but Nina dismissed her with a confident wave.

'She is sister to my sister Magdalena and the one known as Samantha; then there is the other who I sense may be an aspect of me. Between all of us, we have the knowledge to help this man, whom I sense is a valuable asset to all their journeys combined. Nangini moved away respectfully; since the arrival of Hercurin and the Elfling Aerandir, Nina had come into her own power, even though with each day her strength was failing; only the elixir Hercurin left for her, kept her strong.

Working together, Flora and Nina called on the Lady Airmhid for help and, being the Goddess of Healing, she responded. There was one thing she said, they must understand.

'Callum must remain here in this thread. He must grow as the boy Ifor who I can restore and then, Ifor will have foreknowledge of the secrets Cal holds, given him by the Forest Lord. What they have both been witness too may not be forgotten, for they have the identity of the perpetrator and as such, they must bring them to the justice of the tribe, for it is here in this thread that so much unfinished began and here, must be corrected.'

With that, she was gone, as was the body of Callum McIntyre, the man who never was.

In the sacred grove in the forest, a boy lay stunned, his leather pouch had swung across his chest, taking the brunt of the arrow, the force behind it winding him, knocking him out but the resulting puncture wound was no more than a puckered scar.

'How long have I been here? How can this be he muttered, I know I was dead and there was a man who came, he knew the secret of long sight and who the Dark Fae woman is. My parents buried me here and the flowers grew around and through me.'

As he got shakily to his feet he could see the shape of a tall, fully-grown man lay in the bed of flowers, concealed, he looked just as Ifor would when he grew to manhood.

 A tiny wren flitted around the glade, from flower to flower, she flew and the energy spun from her, wrapping around the man, Ifor would become; a cloak of love and healing.

Cal stirred from a deep sleep, his chest was sore; a red, raw puncture wound stood up from his skin in testimony and the sheets were soaked in blood.

In the sacred grove by the lake of tears a boy grew overnight to manhood; Ifor and Callum merged as one and they vowed together to bring the Dark Fae to justice.

Chapter 27

Mysteries

Flora lay on her back exhausted by the events and by the journey through the veil. When she flew as the tiny wren, her name was Bridd, through the veil she was at risk, her psyche challenged by the minuscule brain and the body of the bird.

She rolled over and saw Cal there. In these last few weeks, she learned he was her Cal and yet not, there was a wild streak now and a faint burr to his voice. He began archery lessons with Maeve and his body, already fit, but angular, filled out to full potential, revealing a musculature that almost left her speechless; he was so beautiful. His nut-brown hair had taken on a tawny colour with blond streaks appearing; she didn't know whether it was from the hours in the garden where he worked relentlessly in the sun or from the young aspect Ifor's, more Celtic colouring.

When she looked at him so, she would often see the sheets saturated with blood, as they had been on that one horrendous morning when she thought she would lose him for good. Airmhid's words that he would be the, 'man who never was', frightened her more than she could say and she knew that if that were the case, she would somehow make sure she remained in bird form, until Ifor was a grown man and then, *make* him remember who he was.

She had not realised in the moment of fear that of course, Cal could not be unmade and neither could Ifor, they each carried so much knowledge, therefore they must merge, not just the physical attributes, existing in the man and the potential of the growing boy but all their combined experiences throughout the time-space continuum. Their knowledge, melded in all aspects was remarkable and yet the kind-hearted boy and gentle man, merged to become much more than the sum of their parts. Ifor and Callum forged as their own Trueshape, all aspects complete.

Flora sometimes feared he would change, find another as beautiful as he but the love of Cal was hers and hers alone and the boy who lived within, was the boy she would one day bear; in fact, he grew quietly inside her.

Cal rolled over toward her, his sensitivity felt her response to the weeks past. He held her gently, stroking her belly as if probing her soft inner. Life burgeoned, quickening with intent and Cal grinned with delight. Did she know? Surely a mother would, although it was only a matter of days after conception and yet? He could wait until she did and be surprised at her telling him; he hugged it to himself in joy.

'Come on lazy bones,' he said, giving Flora a friendly slap on the rump. 'I'm starving, I'll cook for the gang this morning, they're all coming over so we can talk about finding the Ravenkin's remains. Sam seems to know where they may be, so we need to go through the veil. It would be good to have Lily and Max back with us too, but I know they have the shop and Max is finishing his book; his deadline's close.'

'Yes food, please. I seem to be even hungrier than ever the last week,' she grinned at him. 'If that's possible!'

She noticed he was closer to Sam now, as if he knew whom the levelheaded one was, on the day he was 'killed' and her anger at the carnage had not left her. If Cal was changed, so were she and Vanessa too. She had become quieter and often asked Flora to tell her about the Italian girl Nina in as much detail as Flora could remember and she was happy to comply. Flora knew from the time together preparing the herbs with Sam for Beltane and Samhain that something had changed within her sister Nessa and that it would soon grow itself into something magnificent.

Now, throwing on a loose robe, she caught Cal looking at her with something akin to awe; she hesitated a moment, glancing in the mirror to see what he saw, Airmhid, Lady of the Herbs looked back at her; she handed her a ripe pomegranate and a smile of rich beauty.

'Is that me?' Flora said aloud. 'Is that how you see me Cal?'

'Even She can't do you justice,' Cal said and taking the pomegranate from her opened it, revealing the glistening red seeds.

'Ah, of course, no wonder I'm hungry!' she laughed, hugging him to her fiercely. 'Don't you ever leave me again Cal, I couldn't stand it.'

 He smoothed her hair, stroking her belly as she felt the tiny flicker of life no more than a butterfly's wing. 'Or a Wren's,' they said in chorus.

Chapter 28

Interim

...worlds within worlds... lives within lives,
...fly swift as a bird... be a fish as it dives,
...smell the soil... burrow deep
...hear the earth... does she sleep?
...nestle in... worming down
...be the bug in the ground,
... be a cell in her skin... go within... go within...

An ordinary day for the rest of the world became a day of joy in simply meeting away from work and all other tasks, under the canopy of the sycamore grove on the hill at Covenstead.

Lily and Max passed through the veil to join them at the farm for brunch. The day promised to hold heat and the subtle rumble far away, a storm later on but for now, they were free to be for a while in friendship, with an unvoiced pact, only after they'd eaten would they speak of the next stage of the game plan.

All the locals gathered first, Cal, Flora, Vanessa and Sam; Beth and Morgan and then Pwyll emerged from Claire's dairy conversion, carrying an offering of mead for later in the day. No one commented on their closeness merely grinned, glad that Claire had found happiness. Harry, conspicuous by his absence for a while; when he did appear, it was with a very sheepish demeanour. Vanessa refused to speak to him; she said she was scared she'd say something she would regret.

Susan and Alex arrived with more food for later, only Robert was absent and fondly missed, but they would see him later that day in Glastonbury.

They piled their plates with fresh eggs, tomato, tiny mushrooms and spring onions sautéed in butter, with bread fresh from the oven. Jugs of fruit juice and large pots of coffee, accompanied note pads and pens, hats for protection from the strong sunlight and a tray of herbs to look at for the rites; the latter items put aside for after the meal, all carried to the huge table on the hill.

Not needing to speak much, they set up; each knew what the other was thinking, such was their bond… all but Tara, who kept her distance, arriving unannounced with Maeve, whom everyone greeted with delight, while Tara stood at the edge of the grove, a sheepish smile on her face. They all said hello to her soberly except Sam, who studiously stared at her until Tara was squirming under her gaze; anger seethed in Sam still. She felt duped, but knew there were truths to reveal today, that might shock some. She didn't care she was who she was but for now she remained silent.

Morgan watched her, his heart went out to her as he felt her pain. Bonded now as Ravenkin and although the change was not yet complete, he knew it would be soon and that Sam's slow burning anger would be the fuel to ignite it. Meanwhile, they chatted, laughed, shared and joked until the plates were empty and the silence yawned, ready for filling with ideas and experiences.

Weeks passed as summer reached her peak, Litha approached, Yule in Glastonbury. Once again, both would need rites worked simultaneously, and this was the topic of discussion today. How they would structure the next seeking and who would be the focus, although it was clear to them all, it would be Cal and Sam; they were both so changed, so clear sighted and of course, Bethan.

Vanessa had some new ideas to share and so, hunger fed, the day began of debate and planning; they must not miss anything, too much was at stake.

There was a pause in the discussion as all eyes turned to Sam who stood up abruptly. 'I need to speak with Robert,' she said, 'he also knows more than he's able to tell us, just as all the 'powers that be' are,' she glanced at Pwyll, Tara and James, 'and I wanted to ask James if might share what he mentioned about the Dark Fae Aerandir and his mother?'

Silence fell. 'Well,' said James, 'that's a great question Sam, but Jamie the Fox shaper and I, are not always merged as one. I have a physical life here in this thread and then I have an aspect, Jamie, who is linked with your other aspect Maeve, Maeve…' he grinned at his own words.

'Hang on James; you and Jamie are one, most of the time, except when you manifest on this thread. On all the others, you're Jamie the Fox shaper and tracker. So why do tell aren't you tracking Sybille like you're supposed to.' Pwyll spoke up forcefully.

'Well, if this is a time for revealing secrets,' James glanced at Maeve, who was listening keenly, 'then why don't you tell these good people who your wife is and better yet, where she is, because the girl I'm protecting is in danger and you know from whom!' James knew he had gone too far but it was too late.

'See Claire,' said Pwyll, 'I said never to trust a foxy lad, didn't I.'

'That's all well and good,' Claire said quietly, 'but perhaps you might want to answer the question, I'm sure Mor and Lily would love to know that.'

Once again, tension overcame the group, so close and so united one minute, then torn apart by all the intrigue and tangles in the weave.

'Yeah, Da!' exclaimed Lily, 'I'm up for hearing that.'

'Actually said Sam, I'm up for the truth about everything. Where my Aunt is, who Cromlech is, who I am in the scheme of things. What my dreams mean, who started all this in the first place. Come on then. I'm up for it.' She broke off near to tears, putting her hand up to stop even Morgan's approach.

'Why Sam,' said Tara, 'in answer to your last question; you are.'

'What?' said Morgan, recovering first. 'Why would you say that Tara, that's cruel?'

'Cruel it may be but true it is, sadly.' Arianwen moved forward in full glamour and beauty, having enough of the subterfuge. 'I saw through Leah's eyes what happened at the cairn of stones you dream of Sam. A block was placed on you long ago and your parents were instigated to do the rest by the Dark Fae; they thought the Fae were Gods. It was not a Christian Cult, as they would have you believe Sam. In fact, it was quite the reverse. This curse has been in place for too long; what point is there if the origin is long forgotten; we're going to remove it now, today.

Tara moved to step forward, but Arianwen would no longer be denied.

'**ENOUGH** *Tara; enough!*' Her horns rose from her brow in one smooth motion; she grew in stature. 'I warned you I would stand up if you didn't at least let everyone know potentially what they're facing. This woman,' she indicated Sam, 'has hurt long enough and has no idea what crime she's guilty of. Her parents disappeared years ago, her Aunt has disappeared and the quest is to find her, not to play silly buggers because the Ravenkin or the Fox Clan, the Dark Fae or **anyone**,' she looked at James and Pwyll, her face stern, 'have their own agenda. It's time, come on everyone. Tools, smudge, candles, salt, water, incense-herbs and something to free the mind that is bound by another's will. Oh, and the scrying bowl too, please Morgan.

'One of you clear the table, please… and Pwyll?' He turned to her expectantly. 'You're not off the hook yet either.'

Chapter 29

Litha... A Cairn of Feathers and Bones

...depths of deep blue... and inky black feathers
...so much knowledge... hidden within
...out in the rain... and content in all weathers
... she will fly far to be with her kin
...when you... she chooses... you will know from the start
...as the bird of the Lady arrows straight at your heart

Vanessa, Sam, Claire and Flora went directly to the herb room. They'd combined all their treasured herbs, incense blends and oils, giving each other full sharing rights in the true spirit of sisterhood.

There was only a matter of hours to get what they needed together and they weren't even sure what that was yet.

'Let me try something,' said Vanessa as she closed her eyes, opening herself to Nina's abundant knowledge as through Magdalena, did Sam; their own wisdom heightened by the contact with their aspects.

'When did you know Nina was your aspect, Nessa?' Claire asked, as they clearly saw a different face overshadow Vanessa's, obviously Nina, but she was gone, deep into trance. She arrived at the cottage in the Between, to come face to face with Aerandir, who smiled a weary smile.

'*Creoso, mellonamin,*' welcome my friend,' he said. 'Nina is within; will I call her for you?'

'It's okay Aerandir, she is indeed a friend. It is lovely to meet you, sister of my dreams'; Nina held out her hands to Vanessa. 'You are troubled and I see there are great challenges with your mother, to which I can relate, but come inside, I sense you have come with a purpose today. How can I help you?'

Vanessa blinked in pleasure at the immaculate cottage and the rows of herbs hanging drying; the fragrance of honey and baking bread was heavy in the air. It was like coming home. Outside was icy cold, snow lay on the ground. Soon it would be Yule on this thread in the weave. She noticed, despite the cold, a tiny wren sat in the snow on the window ledge watching them with bright intelligence.

Vanessa said in her mind, 'Hi Flo,' and the reply came, 'Bridd, I'm known as Bridd.'

Vanessa then told Nina what was happening, all the while, sensing something or someone else accompanied Nina but it was ancient, pure but as fragile as the young woman appeared to be.

Later she thought; I'll look later, perhaps I can help her in turn; the wren bobbed in agreement.

Nina handed the recipe to Vanessa, 'You'll find all you need in Airmhid's bag, although some have been sadly depleted after your friend Cal arrived here; he needed huge doses for trauma and blood loss. Still, there will be sufficient for this rite and perhaps we can spend time; swap some recipes and even herbs from your thread in the web? If I put things in the bag on my thread, they should turn up here, in theory.'

'I would love that Nina. I would like to get to know you.'

'Ah, trust me, said Nina with a small smile, 'we know each other very well.'

Vanessa returned from her trance, wobbly and with a throbbing headache. 'White Willow Bark will stop it,' she heard Nina say.

'Well,' said Flora, 'how is she? Did she help you?'

'Certainly did! Now we need, and this is an unusual brew, honeysuckle, for accessing the Cauldron of Cerridwen, cloves, eyebright, mugwort and mistletoe.'

'Mistletoe,' said Sam. 'Oh no, I'm not over the last lot.'

'Well, it's better than valerian,' Flora grinned, 'pooernie it stinks!'

'There's one more guys, poppy seed.'

'This is dangerous Nessa, are you sure?' Vanessa handed her the paper on which Nina had written the recipe. 'Okay,' said Flora, 'but this scares me. Do you feel strong enough for this Sam?'

'It's time Flo. I can't wait 'til I'm stronger. Samhain nearly killed me, but that was just the first step. I have to know, I'm grateful to Beth… Arianwen, for making this happen, and I trust she'll keep me safe. Then there's Mor, he's not letting me out of his sight recently, so I feel safe to give it a go.'

'If you don't feel up to it, I'll do it said Vanessa.'

Flora and Sam hugged her fondly and then they found the herbs they needed, carefully measuring and blending, chanting together to enhance the strength but to keep Sam open and aware of her journey.

While the four mixed the blend, showered and robed, the rest of the group set up the ritual space. It was Dark of Moon and the air held a static hiss of stormy energy perfect for the working. The day had passed in a blur and the hour approached.

Each of them knew their role, unspoken, unwritten, each would bring a piece of themselves to share in the coming rite. Nothing mediocre here, serious Wytchery by serious Wytches. Robed and cleansed, focused; working only for the greater good of the grove, they cast the circle in the traditional manner, then cleansed, purified and protected, themselves and each other, with pure intent and strong, fierce hearts …they moved forward one by one to add an herb to the brew of sight…

Claire spoke, '…*sage for wisdom, for the clearest* sight,'
Morgan '…*to open the heart and cleanse the night,*'
Lily '…*dittany of crete, the walls to break,*'
Cal '…*and the wisdom to share, which road to take,*'
Maeve '…*John Conqueror root, to courage bring,*'
Max '…*and to take away the fear, the sting,*'
Susan '…*all-heal to bring the end of pain,*'
Alex '…*and clearing all doubt will bring the gain,*'
Bethan '…*to raise the spirits and dispel the dark*
Pwyll '…*add the light of power in the Spur of Lark.*'

Vanessa and Flora circled around the supine form of Samantha. The leaf sprites surrounded her and the energy of Ruark, combined with theirs, lifted her. She floated upright, supported by them, as she gazed into the fire… Bethan approached, handing to Sam a small cup of the cooling, herbal brew mixed into the red tinged waters of Chalice Well, while Vanessa and Flora circled repeatedly building the power, chanting…

'In circle bright… in circle round… we spin the threads on sacred ground… where life begins and all life ends… we summon those whose energy lends… to what we will… that we may see…

THIS WE DO WILL… SO MOTE IT BE!'

For a moment Sam thought nothing was going to happen, she could hear her sworn sisters chanting in high sweet tones. Arianwen intoning, pure sounds in an unknown tongue; deeper tones, Morgan, Pwyll and like a warning,

Tara's husky, sultry voice, from the tree above her. Was she meddling again to hinder her ability to see, she thought, but then all sound faded and she walked an inky black tunnel. Far away, she felt she would never reach it; she could see a flickering light and smell the acrid smoke of burning hair or feathers. For a moment, she thought she would vomit as her fear rose as bile. What if she had to experience the pyre as Magdalena again; could she do it willingly, did she have the courage.

Morgan's face appeared disembodied in front of her; smiling encouragingly, coaxing her on as the herbs began to work their Magick. Then, even her inner sight blurred with a halo of misty white, like looking through a camera lens treated with glycerine. Sound diminished, she could no longer hear her friends chanting and the silence was absolute, but for the sound of water dripping.

The tunnel began to slope downwards steeply and the ground underfoot, smelling of wet mould, was slippery; things unnamed slithered away into the shadows.

Slowly, so slowly, trailing her hand along the tunnel walls through the slime of ages, the light began to appear closer; it felt like she walked for hours. Inching her way down the slope, become so steep she considered sliding down on her rump, she reached a dimly lit grotto, extraordinarily beautiful after the dark passage. Green moss covered the rock walls and filtered light enabled prisms to reflect off the water, pooling on the ground.

Small beings flitted in the moist air and she realised that even here, her sprites accompanied her. Some flickered like fireflies to assist in bringing light to the path ahead, in a phosphorescent, eerily green glow. It led through the centre of the little cave into another and yet another; she could hear a titter of laughter every now and again, which she ignored, not allowing herself to be distracted from the path as water began to seep from the rock walls to create swirling rivulets across the rock floor. It smelt clean and fresh, a spring obviously fed it; she walked, careful not to slip.

This last grotto-like cave, opened into a vast cavern; red tinged crystals sprouted in small formations where the water dripped, adding a musical note to the increasing sound; she could hear water rushing now. She paused a moment, stunned by the beauty of nature's architecture, formed over millennia by water's powerful pressure.

To the left was a small opening to a tiny cave and to the right another; she stuck her head in each of them, but not knowing what she was looking for, withdrew again, preferring to remain in the massive central chamber. Then she saw ahead, slightly hidden by a larger crystalline structure, an entrance to yet another cave; her heart gave a lurch in fear and recognition; this was the one, all her senses told her. Sometimes, even on the Crooked Way, there was a straight line. She followed her instincts and walked into a chamber lit by an unseen source, the floor littered with the scales and bones of tiny creatures, unknown to her.

In the centre of the chamber stood a stone cairn that had been opened, and recently by the fresh markings around it. Ducking her head, she stepped inside the cairn and almost gagged at the smell of burnt remains as if it were only yesterday. Images flickered on the periphery of her vision; she saw who she thought was Bethan, realising it must be Leah and remembered being here before in the vision when she burned as Magdalena.

Swallowing hard, she looked closely at the two piles of bones. One appeared fresh and the other ancient and fragile, yet she could make out the form of a shaper, caught in mid change, one arm feathered like a wing, an arrow still protruded from it, and from the chest. The other pile was humanoid, but she knew from the burnt, feathered cloak wrapped partially around them who it was; Magdalena, her, in fact both, were her. Cal had shown her the drawing his mother had rendered of a slender being in partial change, her back covered in intricate tattoos of feathers, leaves and flames, her tattoos and the shape too, unmistakably her.

Other beings, shapers and humans alike, came and went around the cairn, performing rites; what were they, to protect her or themselves. She tried to hear what they were chanting, but could only hear her own coven somewhere in her head…

'In circle bright… in circle round… we spin the threads on sacred ground… where life begins and all life ends… we summon those whose energy lends… to what we will… that we may see…

…THIS WE DO WILL… SO MOTE IT BE!'

Then Tara was there too, speaking with Leah, Sam heard as if a heavy cloth were over her ears…

'No.' Tara said, *'she can't die, but she must be hidden. Her body must burn, decay as a mortal's would, as it will when left without the animating spirit and somewhere in the Skeins, she must be hidden lest the one who did this find her. Much evil is done; in turn, the one here, whose name I shall not speak, committed a forbidden and dreadful thing. I must hide her or the very web of this realm and all others of her kind will be forever lost and forgotten.'*

Tara appeared to be speaking of the two remains in turn; which was which, Sam had no idea, other than the allusion to, 'decay as a mortal's would'. If this were so, what had Magdalena done; better said what had **she** done that was forbidden and was that also why her memory was taken of these events?

Back in the grove, Sam became restless, crying out questions that made no sense, but which Max as scribe wrote down meticulously.

Suddenly, Ruark appeared, swooping low over the group, agitated, circling and hovering over each of them in turn, then, with a cry almost human, she flew straight at Samantha; hurtled at her like the first arrow out of the Dark Fae's bow, when Rowan fell.

The streak in Samantha's hair seemed to glisten like a bolt of silver lightning as Ruark hit her at full speed in the solar plexus; Sam crumpled over.

Brought back violently from the vision of the cairn, Sam felt she was dying, but a warm wave of musky scented feathers washed over her, within her and she sensed Ruark, open her wings inside her. Samantha's arms spread out to match; she lay on her back on the ground. Her fingers, stretching, became broad wings, the silver streak inherent in the changers, flashed brightly along the side. Her feet drew up and under, toes becoming claws, her back elongating, into long tail feathers from the base of her spine.

For a moment, she lost consciousness, but already Lily, Flora, Morgan and, Maeve were next to her, holding her as she struggled to understand what was happening.

Morphing between naked woman, her clothing ripping to shreds, and her raven-shape, Samantha embraced her ancestry.

She centred herself, slowing her strange, vigorously beating heart, she tried to speak; 'Ruuuark' the guttural cry came from deep within like a sob.

'*Suula, suula*. Breathe Rowan, breathe,' whispered Tara softly.

'Not Hawthorn,' Sam managed to say, 'Rowan, the little sprites are Rowan, *'Suula'*,' before she collapsed laughing hysterically.

Lily drew the remains of Sam's robe over her semi-naked form, tenderly. 'Now we're sisters,' she cried as Flora knelt beside them, joined by Claire and Vanessa.

Tara and Pwyll exchanged a look that held joy and fear combined; the silent interchange not missed by Claire as the others quickly closed the circle down.

Morgan heard Bran in his head as he yelled at him, at Sam, who knew …at the world. 'This isn't right, where's her bracelet! A changer should shape from human to familiar spirit, not the reverse. Ask Tara what this is Morgan it's not right. This is why Rowan died and Ruark fell into forgetfulness!'

Tara didn't give Morgan a chance to ask; she was gone. A Dark Fae female stood on the perimeter and watched; anger, fear and pure hatred seethed within her, but no trace showed on her beautiful cold face, except for a moment her glamour slipped and a puckered scar disfigured her waxy smooth face. She raised her bow, arrow centred but it was as though a cloud came between the group of humans and her. Tara paused to see that the humans were safe before flying on, through the Aethers, heading for the one entity who could possibly end this situation.

With an animalistic cry of frustration that echoed to the group on the Aether, chilling them to the bone the Dark Fae tracked Tara through the silken web of the Between to Robert, where he waited for the Grove to arrive for the Yule rite of Winter Solstice.

Chapter 30

Pwyll and 'The Lady'

...dark lady rides at the edge of dawn
...cross winds blow fire to the waiting storm
...silence is cold as solar storms howl
...broken only by the mournful hoot of an owl
...what lies waiting on the edge of time
...who can translate the dark ladies rhyme
...fast moving comets predict the fall
...as waking sweat bathed, hear her haunting call

Pwyll, a changer from birth knew how to hide his 'oddity', as he referred to it and he was a rebel. He didn't realise the ancestry didn't begin with him and so all his young life hid his identity carefully, yet hugged it to himself like a security blanket because at any time, if he were challenged, he could change and be gone for good. He never thought to ask his parents and they waited.

When he reached fifteen summers his parents took him to see a woman whom he would meet so much later in the thread she lived on; Sybille. Parallel lines may appear to be on the same timeline, but Pwyll met her when she was already sixty plus and in the thread he knew her now, before she disappeared. She was still only sixty-something and he was a man of similar age with grown children of twenty-eight and thirty-three human years.

This made him wonder, because he dreamed of her and so-called future threads, when he was an adult with children, but the bits between were missing then, particularly when it came to his wife. Until one day, Sybille told him the story of the Changers and the Dark Fae who would attempt to kill or maim them. She said it was a rarity for one of the Fae to remain for any length of time in the world of human kinship and rarer still for them to even converse with shapers. Still, his realisation of his wife's idiosyncrasies and her sudden flight from the reality of raising children didn't hit home until she simply started going away for longer and longer periods of time; one day she did not return. By that stage, his love for her was as worthless as the promises she once made; love can die with the flame unattended.

Most of all he felt for his children, doing his best until they were of an age to be aware of the world and what it held; then, it being his nature, he left them alone, more and more until Morgan as the elder, was looking after his sister most of the time.

Pwyll spent months, on and off, searching for his wife throughout the Skeins, which, thanks to Sybille and Robyn, he learnt to navigate. After years of dead ends, Pwyll gave up but now he had a feeling he needed to begin the search again, not for his children, they'd long moved on from her, but for the completely sorry situation unfolding; surely a Fae creature such as she would know more. Perhaps she would know what was happening in the Between, even where Sybille was. Why had he not thought of it before; he cursed himself for a fool.

He sat now, quietly observing as Sam went through her initiation process but something was not right, Bran sensed as he relayed to Morgan that a shaper changed from human to familiar not the reverse. What was going on? He looked around, but Tara had conveniently disappeared.

Once again Pwyll witnessed Sam's resilience; how much more could she take though, he wondered. He remembered clearly, just as Flora described the feeling of the world shrinking as a human body's awareness shrunk down to a bird-size retaining its psyche yet combining it with the knowledge of the familiar spirit. He could not imagine how it was for Sam with the reverse ordering; the familiar spirit having to grow its spatial size and awareness to that of human proportions, not to mention the pain of what he had witnessed as her bones altered. Would this all never end, he thought with a deep sigh of despair for the courageous young woman.

Claire came to stand next to him, placing a gentle hand on is arm. 'What are you thinking?'

'I don't know where to begin Claire,' Pwyll said. 'I need to find her.'

She knew immediately whom he meant. 'Okay, I'll help. They stood looking at each other, Claire challenged Pwyll silently to argue; he did not, relief flooded through him that he was not alone any more.

After a brief pause Claire continued, 'When are you going to tell Mor and Lily, in fact everyone, who your wife is?'

Pwyll closed his eyes as pain flickered across his face; he masked it skilfully but not skilfully enough for Claire to miss it. 'Aww, must I mum?' he grinned; it did not fool anyone.

'You must Pwyll,' Claire responded, 'Sam too and Cal… it could bring them a better understanding of the events across all the threads. Is this what Tara is hiding too?'

'Ah Claire,' he replied wearily, rubbing his eyes, 'you have no idea what Tara could be hiding. I'm afraid I'm in the dark as much as you are where she's concerned. You know the Raven Clan; they're always mysterious; secretive.'

'Well, it's time she opened up. We're not the enemy here,' she finished vehemently.

Chapter 31

Silver 

Silver heard the cry of the huntress, the Fae creature who had haunted the world for far too long. Her essence, altered and weary, she knew that a last bid to find Sybille, to renew with her for a final time was imperative. Something usually so simple, agreed upon throughout the tangled Skeins, had gone horribly awry; balance *must* be restored.

She called the Makers to her, singing them softly in the ancient language of the Making. Her Littleshapes gathered, all but the one who remained lost. Casting their light around and within her, several merged deeper still to within the wounded and void space, in order to protect her from anything else entering there. The taint of the Darkmaker was bitter sweet and they could sense the pain it must have experienced as it fell through the Skeins, pulling the one known as Sybille with it. They relived the fear and anguish, barely able to withstand the imprint of grief and loss it left as it tore through the web; weeping for her with their song to close up the space as much as possible, which meant Silver would remain incomplete yet able to gain enough strength to help in the search for Sybille.

Makers flocked to her to remake the cocoon, attaching it in the Blessing Tree, which shuddered and moaned before settling again. Even here, the blight was becoming evident; a sundered branch hung loose and a wad of dark webbing clearly seen, as more Makers and even Faefolk, gathered to help heal Her oozing wound.

What happens in one place in the Skeins, replicates itself throughout all the web of the Mother like an echo.

Makers and Fae sang songs of mending as Sybille slept on, her spirit fled and her body nearing death, yet still her essence remained, untraceable even to them, but for a discordant note, a remnant, not unlike a cypher, a plaintive, distant cry for help.

Embrace the dark as equal to light… find peace in the day, courage in the night. Remember the dreams and the power of sight… call to us; we will hear you… we will cast out the blight…

As the echo spun out through the Skeins, Nina, Vanessa and Samantha, woke chilled to the bone and disturbed by their dreams. Visions held the sensation of falling; images of the Maker as she fell, frightened, terrified, by the fall and by much more. A ripping sound vibrated the web with a harsh note; a cry of terror so close it woke them, tearing through their psyches, leaving them drenched in cold sweat.

Aerandir rarely slept, his kind not wired as humans were, needed no more than the occasional catnap. He heard Nina's cry and rushed immediately to help. Not something, that was usually his way, but she intrigued him, soothed his anger and healed his hatred; he was changed. A small army of sprites barred the door to her chamber. Once he would have slapped them with his Magick, now he just stood and waited, attempting a song of soothing; he was learning a new way to communicate and the sprites responded with a sweet chatter of sounds. No, he could not pass, but they saw the changes and skilfully soothed his wounded-ness further.

Pulling up a chair closer to the door, Aerandir sat to wait. He could hear movement from within and a sob of grief muffled quickly, had him poised to rush in, but then there was silence except for the creaking of Nina's bed as she rose to pace the floor on quiet feet. Having learnt the new skill of patience he waited quietly, attempting to send healing to her as she did for him, realising she may have given her last ounce of strength unselfishly for him and for the man Callum.

A sudden and forceful flurry of activity; energy raced past him in a blur barely visible. Makers flocked to Nina as she collapsed to the floor. With their focus only for Nina now, even Nangini did not hinder his entry to her chamber. Aerandir stood helplessly watching the Makers work to revive Nina but she lay motionless, her eyes sightless and staring, her spirit fled in horror, the falling Maker wore Magdalena's face.

Vanessa disentangled herself from the sheet, clammy with cold sweat despite the warm night; temperatures soared, post Litha. Staggering out of bed, she walked to the window, the room seemed airless; the cry echoed in her mind and empathic pain ripped through her heart as she felt Nina fighting for breath. She knew, in that brief moment of struggle, Nina had finally lost the battle; she was gone from the world of man.

Vanessa sank to her knees. She tried to cry out for help but she could not make a sound, beyond the tortured sobs wracking her body. Her bedroom door flew open as Bethan rushed in; she had heard her silent cry and came in Arianwen's shape to help.

Light filled the room and a procession of Fae and sprites, moving sedately through the corridors of the Between, approached. Arianrhod, Lunar Goddess of the Wheel, walked in their midst carrying a small flickering globe of silvery light. She nodded in acknowledgement as Arianwen bowed and left the room. Arianrhod approached Vanessa, lifting her chin and with a gentle hand, held the glowing sphere of light out to her.

'Nina is gone,' she sang. 'We could not foresee the Magicks worked by the elder Wytch, La Stregga and Nina's father Eduard Giraldi, who attempted to prolong a life already spent. Who planted this idea in his mind, we cannot know but even for us the Great Mother can have surprises not reckoned with as we walk in separation from Her. Called on as individuals by humankin, we must act to assist while they grow through the same illusion of separation from Her we must endure, as the resulting reaction ripples throughout the Web of Ungwe.

We will send her physical shell to Eduard that he may grieve her passing from this world; perhaps it will teach him not to meddle with life for his own selfish ends.

Now,' Arianrhod continued, 'brave woman-child, are you ready to receive Nina's essence to merge her memories and skills with your own? We do not ask this lightly of you rest assured.'

Vanessa managed to whisper, without hesitation, that she was willing. She looked deep within The Lady's eyes; it was like drowning in a symphony that lifted several octaves in pitch as Arianrhod placed the glowing sphere within Vanessa's open and clean, solar plexus centre.

Vanessa gasped in surprise as Nina's essence merged with her own, expanding her understanding of the nature of the Way. Her memories flooded over Vanessa as gently as the young woman had been gentle. No smear of negativity, no dark thoughts or deeds; in fact a life purely and innocently lived. Within the essence, Vanessa sensed another note that was not of Nina and yet it was and was now, of her too.

She raised her eyes again to Arianrhod in hope and heard, 'Shhh, little one, no one must know this yet; it must unfold as it will. You understand this? We need to appear ignorant of knowing, so the one behind all of these events, and the results ensuing, not be aware. That way, we may well be able to trace the energy of the perpetrator.'

'But,' Vanessa tried to speak, but The Lady sealed her lips with a gentle finger and a shake of the head.

'There is one other who knows this and he too has been sworn to silence. At least you will know when the time comes, you are not alone but you must wait for the sign I will give you.' Arianrhod sent an image to Vanessa that she recognised, the same one she had seen on the stone Bethan carried with her everywhere.

'Does Arianwen… Bethan, know?'

'She does as her Trueshape, but as she explained to you all, there is a natural inability to speak until full truth is known and has become wisdom.'

With that said she stroked Vanessa's face and bidding the Fae to come forward, directed them to lay her on the bed, casting her into a deep and dreamless sleep that she may meet with Nina again a last time in the physical world.

While this was happening, in the room below Sam stalked the floor, shaken and bereft; for her the fallen Maker wore first Magdalena's face but then her own. One and the same, she thought. *But what did we do?'* she cried aloud to the room.

Chapter 32

Cairn of Memories, Well of Tears

Half-light – half-dark… a dove's coo – a dog's bark
Half-dark – half-light… Her lantern still burns bright
Sunrise – sunset… gleaming pearls – blackest jet
Sunset – sunrise… cry in the deep pools… Craft of the Wise
… As Above – So Below… outer light – inner glow
As Without – So Within… All That Is… mirrored in your kin
Half-dark – half-light… raven calls the day… owl hunts the night
Half-light – half-dark… Foxes slinking – trilling lark
No division – under the sun… no separation – All is One

Alma sat in her favourite cave near the sad cairn of bones and sorrow. She sang to the bones while she played with the silver bracelet she loved; sometimes she was sure they stirred. Feathers rustling, hollow bones rattling, she knew who the Ravenkin's bones were. The other, she had a scent of, a memory of her occasional visit to the elder La Stregga on another twist and turn of the Web. She was the young woman who tended the sick girl.

Despite the strange and pretty crystal piece had hurt her head and ears, she had still not given it to M'lady or, come to that, the bracelet she played with now, spinning it around her tiny wrist to hear its sweet notes ringing around the cavern.

She had hidden herself before, as the slender, dark maiden walked the caverns and into her cairn of bones; seeking. Peeking from behind a rock, she witnessed the despair in the colours of her energy and seen the changer that lay within. 'Ah, so yer'n a chang'a,' she whispered to herself, 'Wonda if'n M'lady knows?'

Recently there was quite a lot of information Alma didn't give M'lady. More and more she was remembering other snippets about things and people, events and first hand memories of other threads when she was something else; somewhere else. If only she could remember it all, she knew it would solve so much of what the woman Maeve was seeking; she was beginning to remember her too, and why she sought her out, before the Ravenkin whisked Maeve away from her friends.

Alma remembered the time she had spent with Maeve at the Tuath after she appeared from the Between with the Ravenkin Tara. She cherished that memory of being a little humankin girl-child.

What had happened? Why had she been taken away by the sprites? Why had Maeve been unable to save her? Why did she let go the way she had, come to that, not fought harder to stay with her new family. What had happened?

She had parents who did not really love her. Being a girl was not an asset to them and they'd given her to the Priestess of the Isle for a bag of coin. Bran the Cunningman took her to the lake; she remembered clearly the beauty and kindness of the Priestess known as Leah, but once again she proved to be a difficult, unruly child and they'd taken her to her final home at Scathach's Hearth.

She rubbed her little face with a tattered sleeve, willing herself to retrieve the stubborn thoughts that just would not come.

Rubbing the bracelet soothed her senses, the markings danced on the surface of the precious metal, polished by her constant stroking. She slumbered a little, if a

Merrow can sleep; she dreamed she was a small child standing on the edge of a pond, calling the water sprites to her, singing with them as they danced on the surface, beckoning her to follow them. They had something to show her, something she should know about herself and her origins.

Walking closer to the edge, she sat gazing into the water; the sprites stilled the surface until it was as flat as the polished metal mirror she had once seen on a traveller's cart. As she stared, eyes glazing over the water became misty and she began to see images moving under the surface.

It was Beltane; a tall red-haired woman and a Fox-shaper were dancing the dance, she knew humankin called love and that usually resulted in another child entering the world, if the Goddess so willed it.

The illusion of Tyme passing showed, as the young woman grew round with child, eventually giving birth to a freckle faced little girl. Alma felt the arms of the woman around her, rocking and suckling her with joy; loving the little girl unconditionally and completely, as did her foxy Da. There could not have been a happier memory to recall and she hugged it to her as she woke from the dream, strange drops of salty water coursed down her cheeks; she didn't want to wake up.

Chapter 33
Stolen Child

...sobs and laughter... joy and tears
...the wheel turns on... through the spinning years
...celebrate the seasons... each in their own way
...dance the dance of life... live in the moment every day

The Wheel has turned on, from Beltane in the Northern Hemisphere, to Litha, Lammas, Mabon, Samhain, Yule and toward Imbolc. With life returning slowly to the land, winter released its grip on life and Maeve gave birth to a little red-haired girl-child. She and her foxy-lad Jamie, named her Alma, which meant, *nourishing, kind* and *apple*, in the ancient tongue. Alma was a round and rosy baby and the name, simply popped into Maeve's head. Jamie thought it was lovely; he would rock their new little girl, crooning to her in the shaper's tongue that Maeve was fast learning...

'Caryave, cartel'i-carad caryave, pirya ni lisse'. Atar' elle' cartel'i caryave, quell fa area a' mat nan'. Manke lasteva amin yesta; manke te 'i maksaya helma, 'il a'mat nan' a'mikul, a'lembe n'e ai' pirya kirma, eleaya na' sai nyeer

'Apple, rosy-red apple, juicy and sweet. Da's little rosy round apple, good enough to eat, but where will I begin; where is the softest skin. Not to eat, but to kiss, for to leave out any juicy morsel would be sadly remiss.'

Almost from birth, Alma could chortle, and giggle, loving her Da's voice, his smell and touch on her little round belly, on her hands and feet as he kissed her, singing his little song to her.

No one could pinpoint exactly when tiny Alma became quiet, no longer laughing when her Da kissed and tickled her or when her Mam held her, fed or bathed her. She stopped growing; her little eyes no longer lit up with joy as her parents loved and nurtured her more than any child could possibly imagine. It was as if her energy was trickling away.

Then one day, when Alma was just short of her first complete cycle of life and after they'd taken her to the elder healer for something, anything, to bring their happy little girl back to them, Maeve went to her crib by the hearth to fetch her; it was rare she slept so long. In the place of her child, was a little figure created with root, leaf, stem and moss; animated by who knew what ghastly Magicks it was nonetheless dying, the energy that fashioned it, all but spent.

At first Maeve thought, Jamie was playing a trick on her, knowing his cunning Magicks, but as she saw the image of Alma overlaid on the poor little scrappy, dying changeling, she screamed in fear, horror, grief and finally rage, bringing everyone in hearing range running to her.

Jamie was away on one of his trips into the Between and even there he heard his love's screams. It was the last sound she made and nothing would rouse her; he found her silently rocking the poor dying creature; falling into a stricken silence, a catatonic state. Feeling helpless, Jamie went in search of the entity who had stolen their child away. Maeve's parents were unable to help her, the healers too, and so they sent her to the Isle of the Seers, hoping The Cybil would be able to help Maeve heal and to bring back the child they all grieved.

Years passed and there was still no trace of Alma; madness finally overcame Maeve. She became paranoid that there was a conspiracy; that The Cybil had stolen her child, being childless herself. She became dangerously quiet, eating nothing, refusing to bathe or eat. One day she set fire to the shared hall of the Seer's Isle, before casting herself in despair into the waters of the clear silver lake.

Recognising her from other threads, the sprites took her to them, making her one of their own. Still Maeve's restlessness ruled her; madness claimed her until even the water elementals left her to her own devices. Maeve searched for the one who had stolen her child and her bitterness caused things to alter and change; a dark blight began to affect everything like a choking black web, fish floated dead and bloated on the surface of the once pristine lake. The Cybil knew the time would come when the Seer's Isle would disappear from the land of humankin, forever.

On another thread in the tapestry, a childless couple, Bride and Jesse, received the gift of a little girl barely one summer old, left on their doorstep. They did the right thing, asking everyone if they knew whose baby she was; she was well cared for so someone loved her, leaving her there to give the little girl, a home.

They weren't wealthy folk, but at first, they doted on the sad child, naming her Alma, which the little tag with the image of an apple on it indicated they should. Suddenly and mysteriously Bride's infertility was no longer an issue and she gave birth to several strapping boys, one a year for five years and the little girl languished for love. She remembered she was once adored but she began to wonder if they'd grown tired of her and given her away, as even the blurred memory of her parents' faces faded.

It was shortly after the birth of their last little lad, and at Moon Dark, Bride and Jesse found Alma standing on the edge of the river in nothing but her shift; arms raised to an invisible moon. She was chanting in a strange lilting tongue and the river waters were responding, leaping bright droplets high into the air to form shapes of strange beings with wild tangled hair, much as Alma's own.

This behaviour became the norm and soon the superstitious villagers were blaming Alma for every sick animal, child or crop as she withdrew into herself more and more, finding solace only in her little friends of the river waters, or sleeping in the byre with the goats and hens. Her parents fought over her; they'd not previously had many cross words between them and now she seemed to be the only topic of conversation they had.

Jesse decided without consulting Bride, to visit the Cunningman Bran when he passed through their village looking for gifted children to take to train on the Seers Isle, in the case of the girls, the boys with him either for Druid training or to the Hearth of Scathach for promising warriors of both genders.

As Jesse spoke of the child Alma, somewhere a memory stirred within Bran to tug at the threads of his weave. He agreed to contact the Seer's Isle and to let Jesse know of The Cybil's response. Only a matter of days after her own mother left the thread forever, little Alma made her journey to the Isle. She sensed the grieving of the Priestesses, especially the one who had first collected her; kind and lovely Leah; no one knew that Maeve was Alma's mother yet Alma seemed familiar to her; the Cybil took one look at her and carried her to her own Hearth.

Alma, with her amazing gift for scrying in the waters of the lake and wells, knew immediately if someone was about to visit the Isle. Predicting changing weather patterns, the gender of a child or the goodness of someone's heart with equal ease, she became almost hysterical one day, when she claimed to have seen a lady floating in the depths, red hair spread out around her and she recognised her as the woman who died just before she arrived.

The Cybil knew then there was something else afoot in the Skeins. She asked Bran again about the strange tale of Maeve's child disappearing, a changeling left in its place. Maeve, the promising young seer once destined for the Isle, who met her foxy-lad at Beltane, hand-fasted and gave birth to a beautiful little girl-child, finally came home to the Seer's isle.

Wild Jamie settled into the life of a tribe who accepted him as their own, despite their superstitious wariness toward shapers but destiny will have its way and he left to continue searching for their stolen child.

The Cybil soon reached a conclusion about who Alma was but too late for the child. Being a taciturn, moody, unruly and not at all biddable, The Cybil sent Alma to Scathach's Hearth.

She thought it best Alma not know the story of her mother's end on this thread in the weave, it was enough that the people who had taken her in, sold her to the Isle for coin. She would send Leah to speak with the foster parents and ask them where the child came from but she did not see Jamie again to tell him his child was safe.

On yet another thread in the weave, when Maeve arrived from the Between at Scathach's Tuath, she seemed very familiar to Alma, as was she to Maeve. By now, Alma had regained her confidence, she was mischievous rather than angry or destructive; the two became like sisters. Then fate took a hand again and Alma, as her mother had, gave herself to the depths of the river that carried her home to the lake.

Her anger at the situation and at herself, took her away from her humankin as she too altered, become kindred of the water that claimed them.

Was it memories of the days she sat with her mother by the river or was the memory a deeper cell recall of how the Skeins ebbed and flowed, ever changing and moving?

Maeve, dreaming of Alma's death yet again, came awake suddenly. A memory of what James had said came to her about another Maeve, an aspect of her he loved and hand-fasted, on another thread in the web.

What, she wondered, happened to that Maeve, remembering her note from Sybille before she also disappeared from the weave of their lives…?

> *…fire is harsh and anger sings*
> *…don't go too close you'll burn your wings*
> *…earth yourself go deep within*
> *…let water again become your kin*
> *…let air breathe you, let laughter ring…*

So much truth, so much history in a few lines that at first so apparently simple became a complex thread in the weave.

Chapter 34

Arianwen

Bethan shifted shape to run through the forest; running shifted again, diving into the stream that flowed through the forest close to Wells; she became a water creature, part otter, part sprite. She had been practising this for a while and delighted in the contact with her otter friend Oonagh; time and space meant nothing in other realms.

Her bonded aspect Leah caused the shift to occur and Bethan could hear her gurgling laughter within. Leah was as free as she could ever have dreamed of being, no longer held by the bounds of the Seer's Isle, she could help Bethan on many levels, including in the language of animals and birds, elemental sprites, even the tongue of the elements and the land herself.

A coracle sat, rocking gently on the lake and Bethan could clearly see Leah waiting patiently as Oonagh broke surface. Rolling and diving, she tossed a bronze bangle onto the jetty at Leah's feet. It was the identical imagery to when Oonagh gave her the black stone with the Chalice Well image on it, just a different offering. Where Oonagh found these things, she often wondered. Did she retrieve them from another thread perhaps? Was something like this the cause when one sock went missing, never seen again; she giggled to herself at the thought.

Merging very specifically with Leah to find the thread she needed, she picked up the bangle. She dove into the water again, shaping with Oonagh playfully and then swimming as her watery self, into the caves around the lake and under the Chalice Well. This is where she knew the body of the Ravenkin to be, and assumed Sam had seen it too. Leah showed her the rite of binding in her vision, performed with Tara and Bran to hide the body and banish whatever Magdalena-Samantha might have done to warrant binding. Once again, events on different threads met and merged to create a complex piece of the silken web.

Beth surfaced occasionally to orientate herself, before continuing to the centre cavern where the source of the Chalice Well begun and the cairn of bones rested. She searched for energy imprints of events on the thread when Rowan died and where Cal too had almost been lost. She sought the memory of Tara on the day she shrieked at Leah that the sisterkin's body be burnt, not allowed to receive burial rites nor to be taken, as Changers could, for renewal. Why was that, she questioned again? What had they done? Surely, Leah should know if she had been witness to the rite. Leah seemed to dive deeper into their merged psyche, avoiding or seeking answers.

Lying in the cavern, surrounded by a stash of stones and pretty things, the Merrow Mirdhaucha, once known as Alma, lay dreaming. Her arm dangled in the water. With a start of surprise, Beth saw the silver bangle and knew it was the one lost since the Ravenkin's body was hidden.

Oonagh came out of nowhere; she gently pawed at the bracelet to pull it from Alma's arm.

At that moment, Alma came to herself on the floor of the cavern. Her arm, dangling in the water felt heavy, but she realised something was tugging at the bracelet. Oonagh the Otter changed to a beautiful silver-haired woman with delicate antlers rearing from her brow who with a gentle smile, presented Alma with a shiny bronze bangle of her own, in exchange for her favourite treasure; engraved on the inside was the name Maeve. For once Alma did not fight or argue; this must truly be the Lady, she thought. M'lady's beauty paled in comparison to the vibrancy of the silver haired Fae.

'I am Arianwen,' the being said, 'this silver bracelet was lost and I have searched for it. I thank you for looking after it so well that it can be returned to its rightful owner.'

Alma nodded. 'S'rite,' she whispered shyly, watching with huge mooneyes as the beautiful lady floated through the chamber towards where she sat, surrounded by her stash of jewellery, shells and stones, piled in the centre of the earthen floor.

'What else have you here, little one,' Arianwen asked her kindly. She had already spotted the mesh snood Maeve had made for her; was that the wand Cal had created, but she merely smiled at Alma. Pointing to them, she said, 'keep those pieces very safe won't you. Don't let anyone know you have them. I entrust them into your keeping, until the time I shall ask you to return them to me. Then will you do so; will you promise me?

'Yer, I promise,' Alma whispered.

'Good, then we're friends and I'll look after you, little one. You may come with me if you will. It will be a very different life, but we will care for you. Don't you want to see Maeve again?'

Before Alma could reply, her eyes opened even wider in fear, as she glanced in the water behind Arianwen. She saw, just briefly the reflection of M'lady.

'It's all right,' the lady said to her. I won't let her hurt you.' Then in a louder tone, 'Do you hear me Aelish? Leave this child alone, she is not your toy to play with and discard. *DO YOU HEAR ME?*' Cold laughter echoed through the chamber rattling the bones of the dead; Alma fled.

Beth made her way back through the underground springs and chambers, thinking about what she had witnessed and what Leah had shown her of the images of the little girl Alma, sharing her grief at the death of the child whose parents sold her to the Isle. Bethan was horrified to hear of such practices, but knew human trafficking was still rife on this thread today. Understanding the workings of humankin was always a hard thing to achieve, especially now with her total merge with Arianwen.

Shaking off the disturbing thoughts around the child Alma, sometimes Beth thought, as the images repeated themselves over again, she could just disappear into the Between to be with Hercurin and to live in permanent non-permanence in the seasons of nature's way. 'One day,' she said aloud, 'when everything is renewed; when Sybille is home with us again, I'll be free.'

Chapter 35
Eduard Giraldi

...lives within lives... many doorways of the soul
...even those in disguise lead you home, make you whole
...we are not always kind, when we're troubled of mind
...but in truth it's a game... we're all one... all the same

Eduard paced the floor of his daughter's chamber. Months passed with no word, no sign of where she could have disappeared to. He had been strong for so long, looking after her every need after her mother had gone… now she was gone too; he feared he was falling into maudlin, self-sorry ways.

Was Nina as Fae as her mother, able to disappear without a trace or was this punishment for his meddling in things beyond his understanding.

He dreamed of her, somewhere in a beautiful forest, where she appeared content to spend her days, communicating with the forest creatures and the Nature Spirit who'd haunted his dreams before Magdalena… he stopped the thought in its tracks, refusing to go there yet.

Pacing back to the window through which Nina must have climbed, it was too high a storey for her to have jumped without injury, especially in the condition she was in after Magdalena… he closed the thought off again like snapping a trap door shut in his brain. He would not find answers here, but where could he begin to search for her. There was no trail; Nina simply vanished. Fox paw prints in the first snow of the year were the only sign that any living creature had passed. It was curious that they apparently began directly under Nina's window, together with a clearly male set of prints. He did not know what to believe; her disappearance had nothing to do with a man, although he remembered her throwaway line about a lover, said in jest to tease him. She was such an innocent; losing a year of her life to a comatose state caused by nothing recognisable to the Dottore. Only La Stregga thought it some sort of hex and after his meddling to extend Nina's time with him on the earth plane, he could well believe that to be the case.

He paced some more, as he had every day for weeks when sleep deserted him. He had lost weight and appeared unkempt; his eyes red rimmed; dark circles ringed them like bruises. His hair and beard once immaculate and perfumed were now shaggy and greasy, hanging limp to his shoulders. It changed from salt and pepper grey to white, practically overnight.

Briefly, like sticking his tongue in a sore tooth to see if it still ached, he let his thoughts stray to Magdalena. How he had wanted her; he was such a coward unable to acknowledge his feelings for fear of judgement by society for taking a humble maid as his wife. There again, no one really knew where Nina's mother appeared from either; she had been able to cast a spell over any and all, especially the men. Women never warmed to her; she had no friends, but that apparently had not worried her one iota. La Stregga warned him that something was wrong; her energy was tainted… dark, she stammered, unable to find the words to depict what she instinctively knew and Eduard had not listened then either.

After his wife disappeared, he gave up all hope of a healthy normal life, throwing himself into the care and healing of his daughter, he realised it was after her mother went she become sick. Was there a connection there previously missed? He would joke with Nina that her mother was a faery, laughing with her at his own whimsy, but deep within he knew there was truth to the words.

He often caught Nona looking at his wife curiously, trying to gauge the nature of the tiny, slender woman… he stopped the train of thought abruptly; horrified… he could not remember his wife's name. Alice, Alicia, Aileen?

It came to him in a rush as the air around him shimmered and a figure appeared; she looked no different in age to when last seen, except there was a cold, hardness in her face; her eyes bored into him, seeking to see his very soul. He shivered in anticipation; she had always bewitched him with her beauty… and in fear; the image of Magdalena laughing up at him dispelled the glamour his wife exuded and he saw her for what she really was. Faery yes, but dark and unfathomably cruel… she had left her child, left him.

'Aelish,' she whispered in his ear, he had not even realised she had moved, it was so fast. He could smell her perfume, feel her breath on his cheek, sickly sweet and cloying; her hands were in his hair, but now they felt more like claws than the delicate white lady's hands, he remembered caused him such delight and sometimes pain, her appetites being somewhat strange for a woman so delicate in appearance.

'My name is Aelish Farandirim and I am of the Fae race, yes. Where is my daughter?'

He recovered quickly, refusing to let her close again to addle his wits with her cunning way. 'She is gone from here; I know not where she is. Her friend was…' he hesitated, moistening his lips and swallowing… 'she was…'

Aelish spoke; a sneer drew her lips into cruel lines, 'burnt?' she finished for him. 'Wasn't she a little insipid for your mature tastes, but we digress; where is Nina? She must know about her ancestry now that she has come of age.'

Eduard drew himself up to his full height, towering over the diminutive Aelish. 'Even if I knew I would not tell you,' he roared, incensed. 'You left her, us; disappeared to Goddess knows where. Why would I let you cause her yet more pain when she has...' he stopped, realising Aelish may not know of Nina's condition.

'When what?' she said, her voice dropping menacingly, like a cat's growl.

'She would not want to see you,' he recovered his wits quickly, stepping back from Aelish's vehemence.

'*Where... is... she?*' Aelish underscored each word with a poke at him that sent painful jabs of energy rippling into his gut.

'I do not know,' was the last he remembered saying before he crumpled in agony.

Aelish poked at him with her toe; she could kill him but what would be the point. Let him live out his days as a broken man. She knew much about what transpired, but not where her daughter was and come to that, where had Aithlin hidden himself; he had vanished.

She stalked her daughter's room, searching for clues to where she might be and who had helped her. She found no trace of anyone except a hint of Magdalena, Nina's nurse, Eduard and another faint scent of Nangini. 'So you had help, did you little Nina,' she muttered.

Where was the bag of herbs, she wondered. That would have been a great prize to keep, not that she wished to make herself too well known among the elder Goddesses.

Yes, she had seen it presented to Magdalena and on another thread to Flora, daughter of a *'changer'* she spat the word out. Perhaps somehow they'd worked together; she would love to get her hands on the little book Magdalena had fashioned. She scanned the bookshelves, full of astrological, herbal and arcane tomes, aged and cracking with use.

Walking to the window, Aelish looked down at the garden, searching for some sign of Nina. Letting her eyes go off focus she scried the Aethers for a vestige of any energy that should not have been there. Ah, she thought, a fox-changer, how unfortunate for them. Her shape shimmered and changed again, the glamour slipping as rage overcame her. A red, puckered scar stood out on her cheek, pulling her eye down and the corner of her mouth up, giving a permanent sneer to her face.

A whisper of subtle energy flickered in one corner of the room, but stilled instantly as Aelish turned to find the source; arrow notched effortlessly fast to bow, breath held… nothing. 'I'll find you,' she said to the room before she moved between the threads of so many people's lives. Twisting, tangling and sometimes knotting or even cutting the ties that bind all souls as one in the web.

Alma let out her breath in a quiet sigh, her mouth dry her little heart racing so fast she thought it would explode from her chest. Then she realised that was not possible; she no longer had a heart. She knew in that moment, who had changed her; taken her from her parents, who had left her with her foster-kin and then caused mischief with the village folk before sending her away for good. Whose face, she had seen as she struggled for breath in the water, before the water sprites had made her their own and before Maeve could save her.

'Not a Lady,' she said, losing the pidgin language she had picked up with the sprites. 'No Goddess you; a Fae, a nasty, Dark Fae.' Alma choked back a very human sob of grief. No anger, no fear; something far more dangerous than that; cold purpose, not for revenge for herself, but for all the people she knew suffered at Aelishs' hands and she realised, her own. Was it possible to change the knotted threads created by hate, fear and sheer malice?

Walking to Nina's mirror, she looked at herself, taking in every detail. Remembering gentle hands that untangled her hair, she ran her hands through the red curls, pulling out burrs and snarls randomly. Shaking out her tattered garments, held together by a whim, she wiped tears from her face with shaking fingers. What would her life have been like, she wondered if she had grown up on the thread with her parents. Would she have naturally grown and matured to be the seer, she potentially still could be? How had she fallen into such forgetfulness?

The man on the floor stirred; she was not ready for any to see her yet. She pulled some pretty shells from her pockets and a tiny broach fashioned in the likeness of a fox, which had once been his daughter's, placing them on the floor close to him.

Hearing a noise outside, she flitted to the window; a bier pulled by four grey horses was coming toward the house. Walking beside the bier was a tall, dark Fae who Alma recognised at once; Aerandir, whose twisted streak caused her pain many times, was changed beyond recognition, his hair was streaked heavily with silver, returning him slowly to the forest Fae from which he came.

She patted Eduard on the shoulder gently; he grieved, he loved his daughter as her own foxy-da had loved her, grieved for her when she went away; she was sure of that now. Stroking his cheek and whispering healing words of watery magick, she prepared him to wake up to find, his daughter was home for the last time to rest.

He opened his eyes just as Alma slipped between the veil, to search for Arianwen but deviated when she heard voices she had to follow.

Chapter 36

Jamie's Song

…deep within, lies our song
…twisted threads make the notes sound wrong
…yet here are the answers we seek
…in and out, spread throughout
…in tangled depth… we feel inept
…yet through it all, when we feel weak
…we're at our most strong…

Jamie heard in the Aethers that his Maeve was dead. His despair led him into the darkest places any changer can go, searching for his little girl; he ended up in the glades of the twisted forests Between, where even the Genius Loci no longer walk. Twisted, shadowy places, where the blight was thick with the stench of decay and death and the Darkmaker shivered in fear of the Fae who controlled them. Her little fallen lights she called them, stroking their shuddering bodies, unrecognisable as Makers.

It was the scent of his child lingering here, where the darkest of the Fae walked; he wanted to know how that could be.

On another thread in the silken web, James, in the guise of a modern day man rather than a shaper, searched for notes he heard echoing briefly through the Skeins; one he had not heard in many turns of the wheel. Maeve's faint song and more strongly, the song of his child; strangely morphed and twisted but hers nonetheless.

He was shocked by the extent the blight had taken hold; his time hiding as a humankin was done. He came here to remember, to force himself to let go and to renew himself, as shapers may but found the dying forest instead.

He knew the Dark Fae lived here; he had met one who he realised was actually trying to make his way back to the light of the sunlit forests of the ancients. Aerandir, he thought; how had he coped after Nina passed through the veil? He had seen the fascination the Elf had, with Nina and the growing joy at his ability to feel again, to release the frozen core of himself from the grip of what ailed him. He had not seen the Fae again since that day at Nina's home in the forest, when he took his own grief again into the wilds.

Finally, James merged again with Jamie, to become the protector of the woman-child Nina and even with that, he had not succeeded. She passed through the veil; Arianrhod sent her physical body to her father, but her spark, her Littleshape, was gone into the West; she was free now.

Then, when he heard the dreadful sound of Sybille's failed renewal and the resulting blight, he knew he must follow a different thread yet again. Now he had seen his Maeve and knew somewhere within her the memories of their life together hid. She would not want to remember the pain of their loss; her life as a child had not been an easy one either, but she was actually happy in the thread where their shared history lay. Now he knew they had another chance together. If he could find their child too, then they could decide where they wished to be; on which thread they would live.

Of course, they didn't really have to choose they could move between the threads as often as they wanted. First, there were the allotted tasks to find Sybille, to help where he could with Sam as she changed and possibly, help all the other members of the amazing group, gathered for the same ends. He must learn to be as open and trusting as they evidently were of the Fae folk but he didn't know how to approach the subject of his life on the thread with Maeve.

Stepping from the Between, he moved purposefully into the thread where he knew he could be of most use. He found the group assembled at Covenstead where Vanessa had merged with the sweet essence of Nina; he could hear her song echoing; and Sam with her familiar spirit Ruark. Yet he saw Vanessa was withdrawn, her face, dreamy as if she held a secret to her and not all was right for Sam; the change was not as complete as it should be. There was no sign of Tara or Pwyll he noted; he knew that Robyn would not travel the Between but he didn't know if the others realised why that was.

He was greeted by Flora, calm and centred as always, she too had accomplished a successful, if confusing change. She knew immediately he had made a decision to remain with them to work with the Grove and he asked her if there were somewhere, he could stay. She suggested in town at Earthly Rites; Maeve travelled the threads with Claire, now that Tara had disappeared and rarely slept at Springsmeet, so Flora was sure it would be fine for him to stay there. He was quietly pleased to think he might spend time amongst her things, perhaps work with her tools if she would let him. The answers to all his questions came sooner than he expected when she appeared with Claire for the evening gathering.

Still dressed in her training leathers, she was trim and strong from working with the children of the Tuath; so different in strength and attitude and yet, still his Maeve. She smiled at him warmly, but when he made to ask her if he could use her place in Springsmeet she said, 'Give me just a little while to clean up James and I'll feel human. I look forward to the modern delights of plumbing when I come here.'

Grinning, she grabbed a small bag and head to the bathroom, emerging just fifteen minutes later in a green silk, slip of a dress, her long arms and legs tanned and glowing. He remembered how she looked when he loved her, her scent and feel and the memory was blatantly clear on his face.

'Oooo**kay**!' she said, drawing him aside; a small furrow appearing between her eyebrows that he ached to smooth away with a touch. 'Do we need to talk?' She knew there was something more between them somewhere and needed him to tell her, remind her. Why did it have to be so difficult to tell someone when they did not remember it themselves?

Just behind him, a small childlike shape appeared; it looked like Alma, the Merrow and someone else. Why she looked just like her as a child! She then recalled when she had worked out the connection with Alma. Maeve sighed, rubbing at the same spot James had wanted to smooth for her. Now she needed to sort out where James fit in and how he connected with Alma.

'What?' said James, turning quickly to see what she saw; his senses a little dulled on this thread by the density and the sheer amount of white noise and static.

'I just saw the Merrow, the little girl Alma, who I once knew at Scathach's Hearth and the wilfully cruel sprite she became. She was briefly, standing behind you.'

He saw her drift away in her mind and the pain there when she remembered; it was still raw for her.

'She's also another part of me,' Maeve continued, 'the part I became when I fought for my life as a child so as not to be bartered like a trinket to pay for my mother's drug habit.'

She paused again. 'Alma was sold for a handful of gold, you know? Bran told me. Apparently, a girl child was not always as wanted among the villages as a boy who had strength and could hunt, although Alma and I, were perfectly capable of catching a fish and making snares. It's different at the Tuath; no sexism that's why I love it there and even if… when, we find Sybille, I think I'll stay there most of the time. It's a gift to be able to travel the threads and be where you are most complete, but still visit this current thread with modern amenities like a hot shower.'

James laughed. 'I'm sure that's fixable with a few simple things like a bucket a few hollow sticks and a good fire, but the majority of village folk aren't always too keen to get wet.'

'Yeah, it took me a while to get used to rich body odours,' Maeve giggled. 'And that was just the women folk!'

She sobered as she saw the intensity return to James' eyes. 'What is it? Have I still got a dirty face or something?' She grinned at him trying to still her strangely wobbly heartbeat.

He decided he was not going to hold back. 'Do you remember me from another thread Maeve? Your name was still Maeve and I believe you were more a 'hived off' version of yourself now, rather than an aspect. Sometimes we can have such strong needs for simplicity, we split our very essence in several parts. For you there's your recognition of Alma,' he said the name with a fondness that alerted Maeve to something, 'as a part of you, not a separate aspect and so Maeve may be another such.'

'Every now and again there's a funny little song that flits through my head. It's in the old tongue, I only have bits of it, but I can hear you singing it, and you're happy. I can't see who you're singing it too, but I think it's a child.'

James took a breath. 'Can you sing it to me Maeve?'

'No,' she grinned again, 'I wouldn't inflict that on you; I'm tone deaf I'm told.'

'Rubbish, there's no such thing. Come on give it a try.'

'I won't sing it but I remember this… *'Caryave, cartel'i-carad caryave, pirya ni lisse* …erm …*Atar' elle' cartel'i caryave, quell fa area a' mat nan'.* Maeve quoted it to him verbatim. 'There's another verse but I can't remember it.'

'Ah yes, I remember this; I wrote it for my little girl.'

'You have a daughter James? How come we haven't met if our threads are intertwined as you say they are?'

'You have love, you just don't or can't remember but I can help you if you choose,' his voice took on a burr of accent she recognised as similar to that of most of the Tuath and of Bran.

'Who are you James? How do I know you?'

He repeated, 'I can help you remember. It's not all good, but some of it is and the rest we can sort out together if…'

Maeve jolted physically as he touched her hand. A stream of memories enveloped her of a warm, early summers day and a Beltane rite of bonding, followed by a handfasting; her own and…?

'…It's you,' she said simply. 'I always thought that was an almost erotic dream.' She blushed, looking so much like the Maeve he had joined with, made a little girl with.

His eyes were deep pools of memory if she cared to look, but she took a step back, somehow knowing that after the joy came so much pain and horror. She saw flames and heard screaming; they were her own screams. Had she really set the fire on the Seer's Isle? Dizziness overcame her and James helped her to sit, pushing her head down between her knees and squatting to take her hands in his.

'No love, it's not all easy believe me, I've lived alone with it for so long and doubted I'd ever be at ease with it all but together we can change things; find her...'

'Find who?' Maeve jerked upright shaking off his hands; she was afraid to hear what he would tell her.

'Our girl; our little girl Alma. She was but a summer old.'

Memories stirred, but still would not come to the surface and she heard a rumble the same as when her cauldron used to boil with energy; Alma's way to get her attention. Alma, her little friend at Scathach's Hearth who showed her other things to eat than meat, who swum with her, caught fish, wrestled, built fires with and who had been taken by the cruel flash tidal, river and by the sprites. Then she realised he had yet another set of memories, even more painful than this; shared memories.

Maeve looked at him, tears welling. 'What happened to her after...' she could not finish the words as images flooded in of a small creature made of sticks and leaves that held a trace of a little girl's essence. After that, the leaves blew away as a wind came from out of nowhere; she remembered nothing; only a black pit of despair and the smell of smoke.

James waited a moment until she raised her tear-stained face to look at him and began to sing... '*Caryave, cartel'i-carad caryave, pirya ni lisse'. Atar' elle' cartel'i caryave, quell fa area a' mat nan. Manke lasteva amin yesta; manke te 'i maksaya helma, 'il a'mat nan' a'mikul, a'lembe n'e ai' pirya kirma, eleaya na' sai nyeer.*'

It all came back to her in a rush…

'Apple, rosy-red apple, juicy and sweet. Da's little rosy round apple, good enough to eat, but where will I begin; where is the softest skin. Not to eat but to kiss, for to leave out any juicy morsel would be sadly remiss.'

At first, the shame came. Shame that she had left him to deal with the loss and to start the search while she retreated into herself. It was as if he heard her.

'It's not your fault Maeve. We don't all act the same way under the weight of grief and loss.' He just wanted to hold her.

'No James, it's classically my behavioural history, even now. When I don't want to remember or hear what I'm told, I revert to retreat or anger… sometimes both. Just ask Sam, she'll tell you what I was like when we first started the search for Sybille …at least I feel I've changed for the better now. I'm willing to remember it all. Help me please.'

'I didn't mean for this to happen so rapidly Maeve. I thought I would be able to help you, ease into it as the memories returned as they have to one day for any of us to become complete. I didn't mean for this to become a battle for you again.'

'No, I've been running for too long. I remember my childhood for what it is and that I've grown beyond the pain of it; enough to even let my mother go, to stop trying to save her. It's been me I needed to save, by simply owning all I've been through as a means to learning and growth.' James made to interrupt but she raised her hand to stop him as she continued.

'I became an angry child and Alma, after she was …taken from us, ended up on the Seer's Isle. Due to her bad behaviour and who does that remind you of …they sent her to Scathach's Hearth; it was there we met. She would have been about seven or eight summers by then'; she used the term for cycles passing rather than years. 'We were sisters in all but blood I thought, but now I know why the connection was so intense, so strong; why Alma would look at me sometimes as if trying to remember something, to read me for the answers she was looking for, just as I was looking at her wondering from where I knew her. As usual, I was selfish enough to only think of everything where it related to me …to my dreadful childhood, my loss… my blah, blah, blah!'

She scrubbed at tears, that coursed unchecked down her cheeks. 'Yes, Alma was the cheeky brat toughened by circumstances, she didn't even remember, just as I'd been but I doubt I even asked her what she remembered and if I could help and she never asked, only stared at me with her huge moon eyes.'

A rustling sound and a small sob broke the brief pause as Maeve considered her next words. Like an arrow from a bow, a small girl leapt on Maeve out of nowhere. Fighting first, tooth and nail, Maeve simply grabbed her hands and held them, letting Alma have her way until she collapsed gulping for air, sobbing, 'Maeve, Mam, is it you Mam. Where did you go? Why did you let her take me?' Maeve just held her close rocking her as she cried, while Jamie; yes her Jamie, not James looked on, wanting to touch to hold, to feel his wife and his child, close to him.

Jamie and Maeve exchanged looks over Alma's head… 'Her? Who?' echoed unspoken before they dove into their feelings, joy that Alma was here and grief they'd missed so many years. Crying, laughing and all speaking at once; a family reunited.

As the air stirred and Alma appeared, Beth shifted rapidly, ready to come to Maeve's help if needed but what transpired had everyone struck mute, watching the story unfold.

Each watched; each had a mixed and different feeling that stirred as they realised anything was possible and that nothing was, as it seemed in reality.

Flora and Cal held hands, looking deep into each other eyes and, sensing the tiny being stir within Flora's belly, simply smiled.

Claire saw the interchange and grinned; I always hoped I'd be a young grandmother she thought. I wonder what Harry will feel about that. Flora caught her mother's thoughts and giggled.

Morgan moved closer to Sam, drawn by her smile and by what he felt growing between them, silently, immutably growing.

Max, caught up in his emotions on the realisation that Nina was gone, Magdalena burnt, quietly made to leave; he needed to be alone. Lily's arrival in a hurry stopped his flight. 'No you don't,' she said. 'I'll not let you run away any more.' He gave in but slumped in a chair, head in hands; spent. 'I'll help you find the way to grieve Max. I'm here for you and we'll work it all out together,' she whispered as she held him.

Maeve drew back the better to look at her little girl, whose rust red hair, shot with copper lights was still tangled but she could see Alma had made an effort to tidy herself and her tattered garments, smelling of ozone and the sea. Alma reached into a hidden pocket deep within the folds of her dress and handed her sister-mother a bronze copper bracelet. 'Here y'are Mam, thas'n yours.'

Maeve remembered the note Sybille had left her; it seemed so long ago. Could she have possibly known how accurate it was...?

Fire is harsh and anger sings; don't go too close you'll burn your wings. Earth yourself go deep within; let Water again become your kin, let Air breath you, let laughter ring.

Could Sybille have known her association with the elements, what she would need to do to balance them? Could she have known her need to, 'let water again become your kin,' thus healing her relationships as sister-kin and mother to Alma; Maeve suspected The Cybil would have known, which led her to believe there was an association with her and Sybille, not thought of before.

Everyone began speaking at once, clustering round Maeve and Alma; Cal thumped Jamie on the back in shared excitement at their reunion. Bethan stood quietly watching; she was not sure how this would end after what she had witnessed in the cairn where Alma had kept her treasures. What would Aelish do to take revenge on this little child-Merrow's betrayal of her?

Chapter 37

Travellers

...dare to wonder dare to dream
...when moonlight pools and things unseen
...move and fly on gossamer wing
...as hidden Fae their anthems sing,
...to Lord and Lady fair and bright
...gathering souls to aid their flight
...to places green where Magicks reign
...where all may heal their fear and pain...

Since Flora learned to change, she often practised with Lily until she shape shifted elegantly; two tiny birds flew together through the Skeins.

They could be seen in all sorts of unlikely places, the Wolds, the Between where the Ravenkin flew and in the caverns Sam described. They flew back and forwards through the Skeins searching for the bracelet for Sam and for answers to where Sybille might be.

Visiting all the threads where they knew one another, witnessing more than they could possibly remember to tell about, they flew one day to the cottage where Nina had hid after Magdalena merged with Sam.

A strange sight was the Dark Fae, no longer as dark, who sat outside the little cottage. His demeanour was of someone lost and alone and as he raised his eyes to the two little birds that flew to perch on a chair back, they were pools of despair. He looked at the pair, his curiosity sparked by their boldness. It was not often creatures approached him and it made him aware of how changed he must be. He

"

glanced at his reflection in the window, seeing the heavy streaks of silver through his hair and a face, though grieving, was clear of line or shadow. He was recovering and it was thanks to she whom he grieved, La Stregga Nina.

He knew the two little birds were more than that, he could always spot shifters but now the anger was gone and he wondered why it had always been there before. His Mother, he thought and her hell bent fixation with the destruction of all and any of the shaperkin.

One of the two, a tiny bluebird, hopped closer across the table to perch; beady eyes fixed on his, head cocked to one side. With a shimmer of light and feathers she shifted shape into her human form; he recognised her as one of the courageous group he had been so condescending to before. A small chitter came from the other; a wren, as if to say be careful to the bold bluebird who changed to a pretty, human woman, her face reminiscent of someone; he could not think whom. Pwyll, yes but whom else.

She stood quietly looking at him, studying him closely. 'You've changed Aerandir and I sense you're hurting; did Nina heal you so well?'

Aerandir smiled a little grimly. 'Yes, La Stregga Nina, what a loss to this world although I wonder if I were better off not feeling the pain you humankin must constantly feel.

In a flurry, Flora changed too, eager to console this poor being. 'She's not gone Aerandir, only changed but you know that.'

'Not gone?' he said sadly. 'Then whose body did I carry back to her mortal father Eduard, if not Nina's?'

'Ah,' Flora said, 'that's a kind thing to have done. Her father on that thread would be grieving her loss, especially as Magdalena is gone too. They're both safe now Aerandir,' she reached to gently touch his hand and he didn't withdraw as once he would have, he liked the warmth that emanated from the little wren-changer Bridd, much as he felt when Nina touched him with her caring. 'Magdalena has merged with her aspect and I'm sure Nina will have by now too.' Flora trailed off as he she saw the spark in Aerandir's eyes' she heard Lily in her head.

'Careful Flo, we don't know how much we can trust him, as changed as he seems.' Flora nodded that she'd heard.

'Do you think?' said Aerandir, a little colour flushing his face with light.

'Yes, I'm sure of it,' said Flora not mentioning names; she wondered quietly if this were so, they would need to keep a check on Vanessa.

'Why don't you come with us?' Lily asked spontaneously. 'We can check with Arianwen, she would know, or perhaps Aithlin.' Her motives unclear, except the adage, keep your enemy close, came to mind.

He agreed promptly, relieved at the thought that the young humankin Nina may have found peace and strangely, that he may not be alone any more. For the first time in his considerable life, although still young on elven standards, he was ready to be with his kin and to interact with these strong and clever, humankin.

They took him with them, tracing their way back through the web to Covenstead, just in time to witness Maeve and Jamie's reunion with their child of another thread.

In their excitement they forgot Aerandir as he stood watching through the window; he felt such shame at what Aelish had done, refusing ever again to call her mother. Aithlin drew him to the front door; he bade Aerandir knock. 'They all need to see how much you have changed,' he said, 'but remember, you are not responsible for what Aelish has done, only what you must forgive yourself for doing. Already you have made amends with how you have learnt to care for another and to appreciate the power of unconditional love shown you.'

Chapter 38
Vanessa

...I call down the blessings of a full moon night
...bathed in her beauty ...caressed by her light
...all my hopes, dreams and wishes to her I will give
...for days of healing promise ...and a life truly lived

As Flora and Lily brought Aerandir back to Covenstead with them, a full moon was rising clear and bright, streaming into the room where Vanessa was recovering from her merge with Nina. Beth left her to sleep; she wondered why Cal was hanging around outside the room as she came out.

'How is she,' he asked in his quiet way.

'What's going on Cal? Is there something you need to tell us?'

'I'm just concerned for Vanessa; she's Flo's sister after all.'

'There's more to it than that Cal, you and I both know it. I've noticed for a while something's bugging you; are you okay?'

'I'm fine thanks to Nina, Bethy. Now if my assumptions are right, Nina and Vanessa are aspects of each other, yes?'

'Smart man,' Beth smiled at Cal, unable to resist this lovely man and his intuitive ways. 'Yes the change is complete and I'll let everyone know as soon as Vanessa's slept off the shock of their merging.'

'Is there anything else Beth,' Cal asked directly.

'Why Cal, should there be?'

'I can't say Beth; I'm just waiting for a sign.'

'Ah, right,' said Beth walking away.

'When will it end,' Cal muttered to himself as he stuck his head round the door. Vanessa was just stirring; smiling when she saw him, she looked relaxed and peaceful.

'Hey you!'

'Hey yourself! How's it going?' Cal responded with a grin. They heard commotion downstairs, exchanging glances questioningly. 'I'll go check, don't go away; be right back, Flora will be relieved to see you.'

He rushed downstairs to find Beth confronting Flo and Lily as they opened the door to someone. Beyond them he could just make out the shape of Aerandir in the fading daylight as the moon rose higher, casting shadows across the elf's face; the change was evident but Beth was not going to let him by easily, until Aithlin stepped from the old elder and took Aerandir into an embrace of friendship and evident trust.

A scream of rage came from the forest, sounding for all the world like a Bansidhe; Aelish the Huntress of Souls did not easily let anything go she had her claws into, and now there were several scores to settle with the humankin and especially with Beth.

Acting quickly, Aithlin asked permission of Flora to let them inside, it being her house. Aerandir would need special protection he said, now that he was free of his mother's clutches. Bethan could only demure to Flora, although she was concerned at what he would do when he saw Alma.

Flora agreed readily, ushering Aerandir in ahead, smiling in greeting as Cal raced downstairs. Coming face to face with Aerandir, he stopped short, reading his energy carefully before holding out his hand in welcome. 'You are changed …as am I and the cause is of the same source. Welcome brother.'

Aerandir pulled him close in response. 'Yes, you are right; so what can we do to put an end to it?'

'Stand together; it's the only way.' The others watched the curious exchange silently. Cal never did anything without being sure.

Aerandir looked around the old barn-house curiously. He had never entered humankin houses before Nina's and he found it oddly charming and welcoming after the cold caverns his mother preferred, away even from their own forest kin.

Flora took them through to the huge dining room. 'I'll call the others' she said. 'It's time we finalised a few things and really stopped keeping stuff from each other. Has anyone seen Sam and Morgan?'

'I think they're together in Sam's room. Sam was shaken after Nina's unexpected death and these days, Mor's never far away from her.'

'I'll get them,' said Lily.

'…and I'll get Vanessa; she's awake and looking amazing,' said Cal, grinning at Aerandir's sudden start of interest at the mention of Vanessa's name; he nodded in understanding.

They gathered in to share the obvious joy of Maeve and Jamie; their little girl, becoming shy at all the attention, hid her face in Maeve's dress.

Alma had several items still hidden away that belonged to various members of her new Hearth and was not looking forward to returning them to their rightful owners, although they didn't appear to be angry with her. Would she be able to return with Maeve to Scathach's, she wondered or would the threads tangle again if she did. She didn't know where she belonged; was Maeve, her sister-friend or her Mam or both, she felt tired and confused.

Aerandir saw and felt all that was passing through the creature he knew as the Merrow Mirdhaucha, Aelish's favourite pawn. He saw her flinch when she looked at him, but now he could also feel her pain and confusion, which closely matched his own. Yes, he thought, where did either of them belong?

He approached Alma, cautiously reading her energy for any fear of him; she watched him from where she sat, her face still hidden partially in Maeve's dress. There was no fear there of him as understanding dawned; he had been as much a plaything of Aelish as she.

'I'll not let her hurt you and now you have all these wonderful kin to see that this is so.' Maeve nodded in agreement and Jamie stroked the little girl's hair as he whispered the little song he had written for her in another thread in Tyme. Alma relaxed into Maeve and slept.

Flora brought tea as Morgan came downstairs with Sam, holding on to her hand as if he would never let her go, Sam felt her own pain fall away as she witnessed her friend's pure joy at her reunion with Alma. How ironic that in this thread in the tangled weave, Maeve was a virgin and yet in another, she had a man who patently adored her and a child, once lost now found.

Vanessa appeared, looking radiant and peaceful. Aerandir could not take his eyes off her, sensing Nina's essence was now at one with hers. She smiled at him, blushing at the intensity of his penetrating stare. In her mixed feelings of grief for Nina and joy for their new, merged aspects within, she found herself caught by the power of the little family as they all spoke at once, hugging; drying each other's tears.

What remained now was for them to decide what came next as the wheel turned on again, but first there needed to be a brief respite to celebrate the good that had come of Alma's return and Aerandir's healing. In the UK, it was Yule, which was a time of festivity and they had a ritual of balance to perform there with Rob.

Only Aerandir, Beth and Aithlin saw the face at the window, pale cheeked and drawn the livid, puckered scar on her face prominent as if she had forgotten to maintain the glamour.

Aelish knew this well and decided to pay Annie Savage a visit; time some returns were called in perhaps. Everyone shuddered as the Bansidhe-like scream ripped through the evening shadows and little Alma whimpered in her sleep.

Chapter 39
Nina Giraldi

...in the blink of an eye we're gone from here
...to play in the breeze that blows away all fear
...as the west wind howls and the piper calls
...we follow in the dance, held in Her thrall
...on we dance to the sound of music so sweet
...swept on in the rhythm of Her pulsing heart beat
...through the realms of night into brightest day
... 'til we reach the Summer-country on the Crooked Path's Way
...where our tears are dried and the pain is done
...we dance on again laughing, for we're free, we've won
...though we're battle weary, we fear no harm
...for the pipers trill calls us to the Mother's waiting arms

Samantha and Magdalena merged as one travelled the Aether in raven form to sit on a fence watching Aerandir bring their little sister home. They were surprised that Eduard had not appeared at the rumbling approach of the horse-drawn bier, but no idea of the drama that played itself out in Nina's room or of the little girl-sprite restored through compassion at a man's pain.

Eduard, out cold on the floor, was dreaming of his daughter, as she was when she woke up, restored to him after the yearlong coma; his joy was profound. He dreamed of Magdalena and felt her close; felt for an instant her lips on his but then jerked awake as Alma patted his shoulder. A strange creature looked down at him as he opened his eyes; blinking her mooneyes once before disappearing. He thought he had dreamed her, until he saw the little pile of shells and a fox head broach that was Nina's, given to her by her mother if he remembered correctly.

He struggled to sit up, feeling groggy and confused; a burning pain ripped through his belly as he tried to stand. Staggering to the window, he threw it open for some air and heard the sound of rumbling cartwheels. Leaning out he saw the horse drawn bier and his heart skipped a beat in terror.

Pain stabbing like a knife in his gut, he moved as fast as he could down the stairs to where Nonna was standing with the door open wide as the cart drew to a halt. A strange and very tall man stood holding the horses' heads as Eduard moved to stand at the side of the bier; knowing without question who the shroud covered, he almost fell to his knees.

A shriek came from Nonna as she realised but Eduard, recovering quickly stepped forward to lift his daughter's body from the cart. Strong arms supported him, helping him bring Nina inside and up the stairs to place her on her bed. He did not know who it was, forgetting until after the cart had gone. 'I did not thank him; I did not pay him for his trouble,' he thought briefly, before losing himself to grief. A raven sat on the windowsill, beaked head pressed to the pane watching before flying to land on the tall Fae's shoulder.

'Thank you,' she whispered in the raven tongue, 'now Magdalena can rest too.' Aerandir smiled bitterly and then made his way through the veil, to the cottage where Nina had spent her last months of life.

Eduard had Nina's body buried beneath the old chestnut tree under which, she sat so often with Magdalena. There being no body to bury, he put a plaque on the giant tree for Magdalena.

A raven landed on a branch above his head and he swore to his last day he heard Magdalena's voice speaking to him. Eduard Giraldi died years later on his thread in the weave, an old and broken man. Max wrote their shared history while learning to deal with the truth of their shared threads.

Chapter 40

 *Yule*

In Glastonbury on Yule eve, Rob sat staring into the fire while he waited for the Grove to arrive for an evening of what would usually be festivities. He could see the fire-sprites dancing in the grate and watched their antics as they fought and played for the best pieces of wood to fuel their hunger and lust for life; usually they would amuse him.

Tara visited only briefly to let him know what had happened at the Litha rite and that they were all a little fragile to say the least. Still, he waited, knowing they would come to complete the ritual and to pass the energy between the hemispheres from Oak to Holly and from Holly to Oak here in the UK. He would renew again as the wheel turned for him, and for what... who... he was.

He made himself comfortable for the time being, feeling as he always did round about now the full weight of cycles… feeling old, human and missing his love; his Sybille. They had shared so much, her renewal kept her, if not young then vigorous and healthy for sixty something human years, but then there were all the other aspects she carried, ancient and wise when all combined.

His natural cycles did the same, but he felt the bond to this land beginning to falter and did not know how long he could maintain the energy without her.

Sighing, he grabbed one of her published books from the shelf, laughing at the irony of where the pages fell open...

…Yule the cold is manifest, the earth held fast in winters' sway. Although the zenith of the shortest day and longest night is reached, we know there are all the cold, wet days' ahead even snow, but we are also aware that the days will surreptitiously begin to lengthen from this moment on.

To our ancestors this time would have been one of joy as the light returned slowly to the world. Some of their more perishable, winter stores may already be low, but they would know that the sun's rays would soon warm the earth again. They would share some of the, late harvested foods, in celebration of the Winter Solstice.

At Yule, the Oak and Holly King, battle once again for supremacy. The Holly King has held sway until this hour and now, aged, will be defeated for the waxing year, by the birth of the Oak King, bringing the returning light. The Holly King is thanked for everything learned in the introspective dark days.

It is the time of rebirth for the Lord of the Greenwood, the Great Horned One, who is also known at times as the Sun King. He is born from the womb of the Great Goddess and we can see with this why the Christian folk took this time of year to be the birth time of their own new, young 'God'.

The rite of Yule, which comes from the Scandinavian word Jul meaning wheel, is one of joy. . . even today, when we have so much and do not necessarily rely on our own hard work to produce our food, as the ancients did. . . we celebrate the sun's return; His warmth and light.

Traditionally, we decorate the home with Holly, Evergreen and Ivy, creating wreaths and a table Centrepieces of a Yule log. Made from Holly wood, it is decorated with a red candle, a symbol of light returning and the blood shed at birth. We use a white candle for the innocence of new life and a green, for the growth process of a greening, burgeoning spring to come and the renewal of hope it brings.

We celebrate the change from Holly to Oak King, symbolic of fire and the warmth of the sun's return as He is 'born anew' from the Mothers cauldron of rebirth. We eat a feast of good seasonal foods and of course, there is Wassail, the mulled spiced wine, traditional to the season.

For the Wytch it is a season of giving, not in the way of the commercial traditions of Christmas, but rather the giving of time and energy to a good cause in the community is our way, just as the Yule Log is not a gooey, bought chocolate cake in the shape of a log.

In most traditions, the partially burned Yule log was kept for the year to light the fires at Samhain, Celtic New Year. All fires extinguished, a tall dark haired young man would knock on the door, bringing a smouldering coal to kindle the first fire of the New Year, to represent light and warmth during the approaching darkness; he would also bring a coin for prosperity.

This coin is the origin of the gold; foil wrapped chocolate coins, which many of my generation will remember in their Yule stockings that traditionally have New Year/Samhain origins rather than Yule.

Even the tradition of the gift of an orange, which our northern ancestors would not have had readily, it being a tropical fruit, probably brought all the way from Spain or North Africa, and which I remember from my childhood was quite an expensive item, was a symbol of the orange sun in the sky. The nuts, traditionally hazel and chestnut were also for the children as gifts in their stocking to symbolise the last harvest of Samhain rather than Yule. Nuts, highly nutritious of course, would *be one of the foods stored and brought out to share for the Yule Feast, which is why the celebration of Yule in December is somewhat incongruous, going against the natural turn of the wheel in the southern hemisphere!*

Somehow, our Samhain symbols have also become skewed, interwoven with the all-encompassing Christmas and New Year of the Christian beliefs, which are in origin from the Old Ways, in order to bring people to their new God to worship indoors, rather than in the temples of nature.

Yule gifts exchanged by the Wytchwise are small tokens, a giving of something that we personally love, that we have made or been given. It is then like the giving of a little piece of ourselves as the object is imbued with our very essence by the making and our love of it. We can see today the horrendous expenditure of bigger, better, impersonal and often, hastily bought gifts that have nothing to do with the true joy of giving. A gift without meaning is empty. When we give of ourselves that is true giving, albeit it at times somewhat bittersweet.

Primarily, we take the time to contemplate the coming season, enjoy introspection, dreaming and planning for spring, to mend or make things needed, plan ritual workings and project healthy images out into a cold and in places, violent world. We can feel a little stir crazy; cabin fever is the worst feeling for normally active people. It is important to take some time in a ray of wintery sunshine even if it holds little warmth. What it does hold is Vitamin D, the deficiency of which, in the human system, is creating the disease of our age and within that the promise of life and light…

He dozed a little, feeling Sybille's energy through her written words, wondering again at her ability to cut to the core of what occurred in history; stolen from 'Her-story', in order to create a controlling religion of persecution and fear rather than its origins of love.

Even here, the Dark Fae intruded, peering through the window at the man, she knew, was no man, but who bound himself to the land, in order to remain as he was for the human woman, Sybille Madison. Aelish despised her, more than any. It all started with her and her ability to bring people together, to educate them to be powerful, self-sufficient people, free of fear, which then starved Aelish of what she needed in order to remain young in energy and appearance. She vanished quickly as Robert stirred, hearing the approach of the Grove members and sure enough, they came, weary, for some wounded, and he admired them even more for their courage. Sam in particular he thought, seeing her carried in by Morgan, still weak and sore in mind and body, yet recovering against the odds.

They were all aware of how tired and aged he looked; Vanessa came closer, looking him in the face in concern, knowing they were missing something in the equation named Robert Cromlech.

'When did you become so smart,' he quipped with a broad grin that youthed his face again. He took a deep breath; he could sense Sybille, just for an instance as Vanessa touched his hand fondly. 'What the…' he trailed off confused as he saw them all scrutinise him carefully.

Bethan stepped closer to shimmer and change, searching his energy. What she saw made her step back, bowing respectfully but saying nothing. She transported for an instant to the Grove of trees where Sybille and he presided over a rite, rather than Pwyll; she had forgotten about it amongst everything that had happened. Realising then who he was, as he and Sybille exchanged the energies from dark to light and he became youthful and strong again, wearing forest green. This was not her secret to share but then the moment, broken by the sounds of brawling and yelling just outside, was gone.

Morgan and Cal moved fast, Alex and Max took position between the door and the women, as Jamie arrived with Alma in his arms. Maeve, once more in her leather combat gear, screamed her rage at a Dark Fae female, struggling violently; held by Pwyll and Tara. She tried to attack Alma, her sharp teeth bared. Alma quickly reverted to her Merrow shape, quite able to defend herself, but Jamie whisked her away and Maeve stepped between. Pwyll and Tara manifested out of the Aethers; they had been chasing a Dark Fae female who, although looked a little like Aelish, was not; she was far too smart for that, sending her spies to do the work for her.

Aelish had thought quickly, when she heard the humans arriving. Pulling a wildling from the thread she travelled, Aelish threw her in at the deep end without a thought for her safety and into Pwyll and Tara's grasp.

Aithlin and Aerandir took one look at the struggling Fae and knew, instantly, she was in no way to blame for being there, they could see how terrified she was; Aelish would hunt her down for letting them catch her. Exchanging looks with Tara, they let the wildling go. Pwyll slumped, defeated; he was sure he had caught Aelish this time.

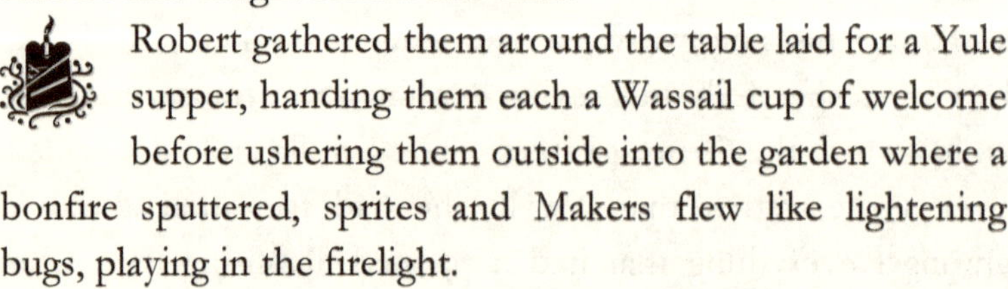 Robert gathered them around the table laid for a Yule supper, handing them each a Wassail cup of welcome before ushering them outside into the garden where a bonfire sputtered, sprites and Makers flew like lightening bugs, playing in the firelight.

In Sybille's absence, he called on Susan to be his High Priestess for the rite, surprising everyone that Beth was not his choice. 'It's a human age thing.' he smiled. 'No offence meant Susan but you are our senior Priestess and this is the rite of Yule, which is not for the young until tomorrow.'

'None taken,' Susan stepped forward willingly.

'While you lot bathe and change, I need a few words with my High Priestess for the evening.' They exchanged looks, but no one argued and one by one, they went to do as he bid. Alma by this time was almost asleep where she stood and Robert showed Maeve and Jamie where they could let her sleep undisturbed. For Maeve it was such a strange yet familiar thing, after their time together at the Tuath to be caring for Alma but now, not just as a sister but also a parent as such. She had not had time to digest the fact that her little friend, she had thought lost to her forever, was right here, safe.

When Robert and Susan had spoken together, they too went to bathe and meditate as the cycle shifted toward the zenith and the moment of change.

They cast the circle simply, Beth and Morgan leading the way. Lily, Flora, Cal and Max, each took a quarter to call in a different way to their traditionally learned invocations, the words appearing from nowhere, written in smoke in the east as Max chanted...

I call upon elemental air as of your currents I become aware. The forces of wind my intellect brings, whilst your music, of inspiration sings. Blessed you are and blessed be... I thank you for attending me...' as she inscribed the summoning pentacle for air with her wand.

Flames in the south shimmered and crackled as Cal called the quarter, chanting...

'I call upon elemental fire you are the flame of all desire, all my natural powers invoke, from your flames and through your smoke. Blessed you are and Blessed Be... I thank you for attending me...'

Droplets of water vapour sparkled in the Western quarter as Lily called…

'I call upon elemental water, I greet you here as your daughter. Your cooling flow becomes still as through your tides my emotions fill. Blessed you are and Blessed Be… I thank you for attending me…'

Finally, to the north writhing vines appeared, as Flora standing strong and centred, began to call…

'I call upon elemental earth the greater part, which gave me birth. Solid, grounded, centred here, my reasons for being, now become clear. Blessed you are and Blessed Be… I thank you for attending me…'

Stepping into the centre, they formed a circle facing out to call to the spirit of Aether to attend their rite, spun the energy sunwise…

'We call upon Spirit, elemental Aether, with our inner-selves cleansed, we hear you whisper, through the flow of lymph, and the blood in our veins we ask you to ward us from all fear, all pain. Blessed you are and blessed be… we thank you for attending, as we did will, SO MOTE IT BE!

The Australian born all felt a little awkward adapting energetically to the different directions in the northern hemisphere, despite the workings performed before, but Robert smiled happily at them when they were finished.

They had expected to perform a complex rite, but Rob had them sit in the circle facing the altar of earth in the north; for it is from here in the northern half of the planet the cold, winds blow.

In deep tones, he guided them in meditation…

'I am taking you on a journey where you may make contact with the energies and mysteries of life in death and in rebirth; whatever that means to you personally and what can be revealed to you and you

alone can understand.' He paused a moment giving them time to relax into a deeper space within before continuing…

'You find yourself standing at the entrance to a dark cavern,' at which he heard Sam's sharp intake of breath, but he did not pause; it would be what it must.

'A velvet blue night is filled with stars but Lady Moon is not visible. You can sense the energy of nature around you, rocks and trees take on larger forms, but you are unable to see clearly in the dark; your sense of smell is acute. Breathe the scent of loamy soil and mossy green; notice anything else that takes your attention.'

Lily could smell violets and thought of her mother's perfume; for Morgan it was a morning mist in Wales as a child. Sam could smell parchment, ink and her Aunt's energy. Vanessa could smell the cottage where she had spent a little time with Nina, and Flora the bag of herbs Airmhid had given her; for Cal it was his father's library and the leather chair he had loved. Max found himself transported by the scent of a warm Italian summer's day and for some reason, shelled peas. All received a scent they knew and recognised, even Tara, observing with Pwyll and Claire from the tree above, shifted to moments in their changers lives when scents had meant life or death to them.

Roberts's voice continued, picking up the pace…

When you feel ready, walk into the cave. Although it's dark, the walls are smooth and you're able to guide yourself by touch into the depth of the cavern. You feel safe and the cave is warm; you have the sense of returning to the womb as you feel the cavern floor sloping downwards deep into the earth. Notice the smells that come to you on the air; notice there is a light, becoming a brighter,' once again, Sam was back in the cavern where she had visited the cairn of bones.

Phosphorous light emanates from the walls and floor, revealing more of your surroundings as you continue moving, deeper still, into the

*earth. Ahead, as you round a bend, the light strengthens and you can see
something awaiting your attention. I'll leave you a moment to see and
connect with what awaits you there.'*

Each of them made their way deep into the heart of
the Mother; all except Sam, who once again relived the
journey to the cairn of bones and sat weeping for she knew
not what… lost and alone in the darkness; the light had not
manifested for her.

'When you are ready,' Robert's voice reached them from
far away, *'return to the everyday world and to your circle of friends.
Some of you may carry a Yule gift to cherish; perhaps it won't be evident
as to why this gift was given to you but trust that it will reveal itself in
time. Journey back the way you came and I'll give you time to get your
bearings again.'*

When all had returned to everyday awareness,
blinking in the torch and firelight, Rob knelt at
Susan's feet as she wielded a sword of intricate
design, which appeared to shimmer in her hands and yet was
large enough to be far too heavy for her to wield. It was
almost like watching a ritual of knighthood enacted, but the
exchange of energy shone from the sword and into Rob's
chest; it spun out in arcs to cover his body until he was
almost invisible to their eyes. As the light dimmed Robyn
Goodfellow, arrayed in forest green stood there, youthful and
smiling until Rob's features settled again into his accustomed
physical persona, younger, however, his wrinkles smooth; his
thick, silver hair, curled to his shoulders. He shook himself as
Susan, still holding the sword, stared open-mouthed at his
transformation. Rob laughed aloud, taking the sword from
her nerveless fingers; he kissed the blade and laid it on the
altar with ritual respect.

He turned to the Grove, all but one with a smiling face, and declared, 'Let the feasting begin,' to which Susan returned, 'Let the wine also be Blessed,' as she led the blessing of the Wassail, in which Rob place a couple of drops of his amber nectar, to be passed around with kisses exchanged and moon cakes to share.

Together they said farewell the elements and all other gathered souls and went inside to the Yule feast. Now was the time they could ask their questions and share their experiences into the early hours. Only Sam held back, Tara and Pwyll watched her closely and Morgan wanted only to hold her and make right whatever it was she felt she could not share.

Vanessa received a key as her Yule gift and was excited to know what it would open. Aerandir and Aithlin had stood outside the circle during the rite to keep watch; Rob invited them to stay for the feast. Aerandir asked if he could see the key, which she showed him. He said it might be the key to Nina's little cottage; he shared this with her whilst thinking, '… and the key to my hopes'.

Morgan and Cal had both received bone-handled knives with curved, Druids' blade and Max, a parchment that he could not read, it being in a strange text. Aithlin said he could help him with it. Maeve, given a vision of the snood she had made for Beth; reminded her, she had not seen it recently. Flora a plant she could not identify first off, but giggled when she realised it was Chaste tree '… a bit late for that,' she whispered to Cal. Bethy received a jog to her memory like a physical tap on the head, about the silver bracelet; she didn't know why she kept forgetting its significance. When she was in her Arianwen aspect, everything was clear but as Beth, she was just that, Beth.

They quizzed Robert about the vision they had all clearly seen and without hesitation, he shaped to his Robyn form …Robyn Goodfellow, friendly, joyful, woodland sprite who held the balance of the land between the cycles for the Lord of Nature. He sported small horns, laughing and mischievously playful and known in other cultures, as Pan the Goat-foot God, Dionysius, Bacchus, Tehmut and by many other names. In the British Isles he was the Spirit of the Land of Albion along with his Lord, Herne the Hunter. He held the promise of spring's return and in autumn, an abundant wine harvest.

Finally, Sam spoke, 'So you were my Aunt's lover?' she queried. 'Are you the reason there was never anyone else; why she was single all her life?'

'Yes and her friend,' he replied simply, 'and still am; I only wait her return from renewal and I know this will happen. We are what you might call twin souls; that is to say one soul living in two physical bodies on the same thread.' He continued to tell the story of the Birthing Tree and the renewal of souls, willingly conscious, who have gone beyond the single identity of their ego persona to embrace all aspects of self until they become unified, whole. Sybille is the aspect Silver has waited for and Silver is as much Sybille, as Sybille is Silver. They blinked in unison at his words, trying to understand the nature of such a consciousness.

'You would know Bethy and you Cal, Vanessa, Morgan, Maeve… you've all found those aspects and bonded with them. They still exist where their threads wind through the Skeins, just as you continue on here. When you become fully conscious, cease to fight the larger portion of you, which is pure spirit, you will understand that there are multiple aspects roaming through the web of Ungwe both conscious and unconscious of your existence too. It's not only here on this earth thread we lose our way; there are many ways we can go astray,' he glanced at Sam but she would not meet his eyes.

'It would be so much simpler if we could just be reminded of this when we fall into unconsciousness,' said Vanessa.

'Don't you think the nudges you've been getting recently are indicators of something trying to get your attention?' Rob roared with delight. 'Or would you like a more 'in your face' kind of wake-up call?'

'Erm… nope… I think we get the drift,' Lily giggled.

Soon it was clear they would have to make their way back to their thread on the loom… tomorrow was another day and it was a working one. They had clients, customers to attend to, and an evening of music at the Harvest where they were performing for a small gathering. Home and bed were the unanimous decision. Robert kissed the girls good night, with gruff hugs for the men as they thanked him for sharing so openly.

'This has to be the most anyone has told us during the whole process,' said Sam, feeling the best she had felt in ages.

Chapter 41
Just Another Morning

...eyes... the window to the soul
...look within to see the whole
...of the inner heart and busy mind
...leave the ego self behind
...deeper still in the world inside
...where are you there... or do you hide
...from other's stares or a wayward glance
...straightening shoulders... taking a stance
...do you trust who lives in there
...let them out... show yourself... do you dare?

In the morning, Sam woke up, drained and teary; the relaxed ease of the night before diminished again. She wondered how she would face a day at the desk and Annie's sneering, scrutiny. Rob had placed a small vial of his elixir in her hand at the end of the night. 'For when you feel frail or afraid,' he had whispered to her, stroking her cheek fondly.

Since she had merged with Ruark, she had not seen her familiar spirit again, but she could feel her as if locked away inside her, trapped; had that been the plan she wondered and whose? Where was Rowan? Sam's gut ached physically; she could feel the beautiful raven flapping her wings inside her, a prisoner in a cage of ribs. Sometimes her arm and chest ached from where the arrows had pierced her. She knew that was not right, but not how to heal it or how to make amends for an offence, she had not known she had committed.

From everything, she had read in Sybille's notes and from talking with Claire, Lily, Flora and Morgan, this whole initiation process was all wrong somehow and nothing like anything experienced. Tara was avoiding her; in fact, she was conspicuous by her absence, as was Pwyll, just when she most needed to speak to their experience.

Morgan was wonderful, always there for her, as of course were her closest friends but they were all happy, despite the situation with Sybille still unresolved and she didn't want to be constantly the proverbial fly in the ointment.

Stretching her aching body, she placed her hands over the strange fluttering feeling under her ribs. Breathing deeply she attempted to free up what felt like a stitch as if she had been running hard. Her little vial from Rob seemed to flash at her from where it sat on the dresser; she unstoppered it, carefully measuring a drop onto her tongue. Warmth and sweetness rushed through her; fire and earth she thought with an aftertaste of ozone and a scent of honeysuckle. For some reason her rhyme from her Aunt came to mind…

…earth you are, from earth you came… your intellect from air you gain… your fire should burn, with flaming ire… yet water has put out your fire…

…all those elements, present in one small drop of liquid music that vibrated her own essence to the core.

Feeling alert and refreshed, 'Robert should patent that,' she said to her stirring sprites with a grin. They hummed with their version of delight. Sam was beginning to understand every nuance of their song and could not remember clearly, when they had not been with her, in fact she knew they had always been there, albeit unseen. Since her session with Tara, what she had seen then, and the more recent experiences, she was beginning to understand much more about the past.

What most disturbed her was the sense that her parents were still alive. She would catch glimpses, when scrying for something totally unrelated; see images of them going about their daily tasks in what appeared to be a community of some sort. It appeared to revolve around a lot of discipline and oath taking, initiation and worship, of what she could not say.

Moving to the window, she saw the day dawning bright and clear, a hint of moisture rose from the ground in misty tendrils and crickets were singing. There would be a storm by the end of the day, for sure; and welcome after the summers' intense heat.

Sam showered and dressed feeling ready for another day. Picking up her hairbrush, she paused to look in the mirror; Sprites wrestled it from her hand. This was a regular morning game, where she pretended reluctance and the sprites giggled and fought for it; she let them win, enjoying their administrations as much as they enjoyed the game. Sometimes she envied their innocent playfulness tempered by their fierce protectiveness of her.

Her tangled hair had thickened and changed; this morning the sprites restored it to a satin shine before braiding little items in it and creating wild elflocks around her face. Her tattoos showed, bright colours in the morning light, contrasting against the silvery streak of hair, but just as the elder tree outside her window was showing ripened clusters of burgundy coloured berries so too did her tattoos begin to mirror the change of season to come. Some showed the beginning of amber and gold leaves as the sun had reached its zenith and began the descent toward autumn.

Shivering, she thought of the word descent and Robert or, better said, Robyn's guided journey into the caverns of their mind. For her, back to the cave of bones and feathers, where Magdalena's remains were now no more than a pile of ash.

She put her hand on her chest to still her breath and strangely beating heart; it reminded her of when she had shifted shape to become raven. In that instant she realised what had been wrong, first she needed to merge with Rowan and then make the shift. Where was Rowan's bracelet? On her own, it would not work because an important piece of the puzzle was missing. Come to that, where was Rowan?

With a sigh, she thanked the sprites and went to find some breakfast. It was still early; she restlessly paced the verandah gnawing on a crusty, buttered slice of bread, as the sun rose fully on what would become a blistering hot day until the storm broke later. Suddenly Silver floated into view, her attendance of Makers now numbered, as many Dark as there were Light. It had the appearance of her leaving a trail of black blood behind her, relieved only by flashes of silver-lit Makers.

Helplessly Sam watched and felt the despair creep back into her heart.

Chapter 42
Lost Cycles... New Battles

A week later, Sam arrived at work, a little earlier than the others did; she had taken to waking early and going in, in the quiet of the morning. She was surprised to see Annie Savages' car in the parking lot. Always on time but never early, Sam immediately felt something was not right.

She was carefully quiet as she opened the door at the rear of the building. Voices floated on the air, chanting, muttering; sounding like incantations in a strange tongue and she thought she could hear the beating of great wings. Goddess knew she should be used to strange languages by now.

Moving soft footed down the hallway to the meditation and circle space, she paused; it reminded her of the time she had witnessed Sybille and her coven members performing a rite of seeking, letting Beth in the door but not her.

Sound, echoed strangely in the building at the best of times, there being so many rooms within rooms, stairwells and hallways, but it was as if one moment it was very close to where she stood, then the sounds would whip around her and come from a different direction entirely. It was rather disorientating, to say the least.

A muffled yelp brought her back to the moment, followed by running feet and a door slamming. Several of Annie's sycophants, one-time members of Sybille's' teaching Grove, burst out of the Circle Space and came to a screeching halt as they saw Sam standing in the hall.

'Where's Annie?' said Sam crossly.

'She's… erm, she's in the ritual room Sam. Something's not right. She's been behaving strangely for months, seeing and talking to something we can't see, but now we've had enough of her ego and her irrational carrying on and with that, they raced outside just as Beth was coming in.

Beth, restless too, had decided to finish off some pieces she was weaving for customer orders; with everything that had happened she was unusually behind with her work. She grabbed the sleeve of one of the running women, but shaken off by her, called out, 'Whoa, where's the fire,' disgruntled to have a pack of people running through the business at this time of the morning with no scheduled meetings in the book that she knew of. Nothing gave Annie the right to use the premises without notifying Flora, Sam or herself.

Spotting Sam walking toward the open door of the room quietly, now that the noise of the women leaving had gone, Beth could hear the strange incantations coming from there too. She sent a message to Sam, telepathically letting her know she was there so as not to startle her as she came up behind her.

Sam turned with her finger to her lips as she beckoned Beth closer. What they saw as they looked in filled them with despair. Sticky black web festooned every surface; small creatures and birds hung suspended and the strange susurrus incantation continued. Refusing to be intimidated in their own space, they called out into the Aethers to Tara, Pwyll… anyone to come; Sam stepped inside; the stench was almost overpowering.

Bethan shifted shape, bringing all her attention to the figure, crouched whispering into Annie's ear, as she lay unconscious on the Altar. Her colour blanched a sickly yellow, mouth slack… open in a silent scream.

Rage overcame Sam at that moment and if it weren't for Beth, she would have fallen on the Dark Fae. Arianwen, fully manifested, pushed Sam behind her, not to protect but to stop her attacking the crouched Fae female. Drawing herself to her full height, Arianwen approached her; there was fear in the Dark Fae's eyes, caught in the act of stealing back the energy she had spent in giving Annie the appearance of youth.

'Your cowardice knows no bounds,' Arianwen sang, her voice cool and soothing despite her demeanour. 'This time you go too far, entering a sacred space uninvited and attempting harm to a humankin.'

'I **was** invited,' hissed the Fae, 'this one is mine. She dedicated herself to me long ago. I gave her much and she has failed me. I only take back what is mine. Arrogant Wytch; she thought I was The Morrigan herself, no less.'

Annie stirred, groaning, but meeting the eyes of the Fae still leaning over her, fainted.

Sam, by this time had had enough and stepped from behind Arianwen, her sprites again surrounding her, fiercely protective yet obviously terrified; the fear that flared in the Dark Fae's eyes was unexpected as with a scream, she vanished. Web and creatures collapsed, drawn into the void of her leaving; the stench of decay remained.

Beth and Sam sighed with relief, rushing to Annie's side. Two high points of colour flared on Annie's cheeks, but her skin remained slackened and new furrows had appeared around her mouth; her eyes were dark rimmed and sunken.

While Beth chafed her hands to bring warmth to them, Sam fetched cold cloths; she placed one on Annie's forehead and wiped her pallid skin. Annie stirred, but began to shake as shock set in; tears trickled from her closed eyes, which Sam gently dried, her compassion melting her anger.

'We need some rescue remedy,' said Sam, 'I'll fetch it; I know where Flora keeps some for staff and clients.'

Beth moved around to Annie's head, taking the woman's head into her lap and pouring song, sweet as an elixir into her energy field. As Sam made to go, she fumbled in her jacket pocket, extracting the little vial Rob had given her. 'What am I thinking of? This is worth more than any herbs combined to help Annie.' She dripped one tiny drop into the corner of Annie's mouth.

Restoration was immediate and violent as Annie sat bolt upright and deposited her breakfast and anything else remaining in her stomach onto the floor. Sam barely had time to move her hand away.

'What …what in the world's going on?' Annie cried, gagging at the stench of her own vomit. 'What happened to me, why am I here at work?'

Beth soothed the frightened woman with a small song of mending as Annie struggled but failed to stand.

'It's okay Annie, you fainted,' said Sam, thinking fast. 'Did you have breakfast? 'What do you remember about this morning?'

'Well,' Annie's brow creased with concentration, 'I came in to do the rosters for Sybille. You know what a stickler she is for everyone getting their hours in for the month on time.'

Sam and Beth exchanged glances, not missed by Annie. 'What's wrong?' she asked.

'Annie, what day is it?' Beth asked her gently.

'Er, well… it's Wed… no Tuesday 15th April and soon Sybille will be going to her writer's retreat in the UK.'

Sam swallowed hard, 'It's just past Litha, Annie and Sybille has…' Beth jumped in quickly before Sam could finish. '…And Sybille has already left Annie, don't you remember? She left early this year and has taken an extended sabbatical to finish her latest books. She left Sam, Flora, Maeve and me to work from here and help take the burden off you, now you're only working part-time but if you're not well, we can manage. There are things you can do from home to help us if you need the extra hours, but after you're fainting like this today, I really suggest you go to an herbalist, perhaps Flora.'

Annie looked at Beth, then Sam in confusion. 'Well, I do feel a bit strange and, what did you say Sam… it's Litha? That would mean, it's December and I've,'… she trailed off, 'lost a few months,' finished Beth for her, kindly. 'Perhaps you're just over tired; we have worked you hard lately. Anyway, let's get you home, I'll drive you in your car and walk back. Okay?'

Annie nodded tearfully as Beth and Sam helped her to her feet, looking at the mess on the floor in embarrassment.

'Don't worry, I'll clean that up,' said Sam, helping her to a chair. Annie handed Beth her car keys without a word in fact, her passivity was more than unusual. Together they sat Annie in the waiting room at the reception; Sam casually walked with Beth to the door as she left to get the car.

'We need help on this one Beth. How will we explain to Annie that Sybille's been gone coming up to two years at Lammas and that she's the victim of her own ego and the exploitation of a crazy Dark Fae and been a mega bitch who stole Claire' husband, although I think that may have been going on before any of this debacle.'

'If it weren't so tragic I'd laugh at that statement Sam,' Beth giggled, and then sobering, said, 'it is what it is and she will have to be accountable for her part. She could only *be* exploited, because of her ego. What we do about her memory loss, I don't know, but I'm sure between you, Flo and Nessa you'll come up with a remedy, though I kind of like the new docile Annie,' She grinned again. 'As to what Harry will do or say when he sees her like this? I guess what goes around, comes around, eh?'

Sam went back to sit with Annie while they waited. 'So, dear,' said Annie sweetly, 'I'm sure you'll be missing your Aunty but if you need a chat with an older woman, I'm always available with a listening ear.' Saved by Beth's return, Sam did not have to reply. As Beth led Annie to her car Sam stood at the door, the others were just arriving.

She muttered to herself, 'Who are you and what have you done with Annie Savage?' She smothered a giggle as Morgan reached the door.

'You look happier today love,' he said, 'what's so funny?'

'Ah, well… I'll wait 'til everyone's here and tell you all together.'

'Fair enough,' Morgan replied, drawing her into a warm hug. 'At least it's made you smile again and brought colour to your cheeks.' Dozens of sprites surrounded them both like a cloud.

Chattering and laughing, everyone arrived to start an ordinary day in an extraordinary situation. Even Sam felt better after the trauma of the past weeks; her relationship with Morgan was one of the things that constantly sustained her. Litha was past; Yule in the northern climes; what next.

Cleaning she thought, just as Vanessa appeared, mop and bucket in hand, the water steamed with fragrant herbs and the tangy scent of citrus.

'I'll do that Nessa,' said Sam, 'and it's going to take more that this to clean the circle.'

'It's okay, I'll get this, but what happened?'

Sam took the mop from Vanessa's hand as Beth came back from seeing Annie home. 'Come with me a minute Nessa there's something you need to know.'

'Okay, you sound serious Bethy, what's going on?'

Beth told her what had happened and Vanessa sat quietly before replying. 'Was Harry there?' she asked.

'Yes, but I'm not sure how long for, he took one look at your mother and freaked out but then helped me get her to bed. He actually said he had been there because she had wanted to speak to him as a doctor. Even now, he can't be honest, but that's unimportant. He said he had a tight schedule and would be heading back to Melbourne for a few days, so I called in on her neighbour who said she would keep an eye on her after he left.'

'I'll call round later when I'm sure he's gone,' said Vanessa, 'I really don't want to see him.'

'I'll come with you sis,' said Flora, she had bumped into Sam in the hall, 'then we can assess what needs to be done.'

'Okay, thank you. I'd rather not face this alone actually, but it is a worry. Fainting I can understand from what Sam and Beth described… I'd probably have wet myself if that Dark Fae was hanging over me like a vampire… but for her Mum to forget what day it is… that's a serious concern. Do you think the Fae made her forget so as not to tell about her hand in everything that's happened?'

'Most likely from what we know of her. I keep forgetting her name, oddly… as if I'm not supposed to remember it,' said Flora. 'I have to remind myself. I guess it's a bit like Beth saying, when she's merged as Arianwen she remembers, but as Beth, her human side kicks in.'

Beth came from reception at that moment, concern written on her face. 'Nessa, you have to go now; Annie's neighbour just rang. She went in to see your mum after Harry left and could not wake her up; she seems to have fallen into a coma. There's an ambulance on the way so you might want to go straight to the hospital. Come on, I'll drive you. I'm the only one without appointments today.'

Vanessa stood still, looking utterly stunned. Flora reached out to her, gently taking her in her arms. Over her sister's head, she said quietly. 'You take her Beth but I'll clear my schedule, there's one waiting for me now but the rest, are all repeat clients, nothing that can't wait a day; then I'll go to the hospital. Sam, can you reschedule them please I'm sure they'll understand.' She gave Vanessa a quick squeeze of encouragement. 'It's probably just exhaustion and the fact that I haven't seen her eat recently. She's in good hands anyway sis.'

Beth drove to the hospital with Vanessa in silence; no words could help the obvious concern and fear written all over the younger woman's face.

Inside Vanessa was calling out to Nina for help, but there was only silence and a gaping void of fear for her mother.

Chapter 43
Storm Front

... In the blink of an eye we go from here
...to play in the breeze that blows away our fear
...as the west wind howls and the piper calls
...we follow in the dance; held in Her thrall
...on we dance to the sound of music sweet
...swept on in the rhythm of Her pulsing heart beat
...through the realms of night into brightest day
...'til we reach the Summer-country on the Crooked Path's Way
...where our tears are dried and the pain is done
...we dance on again, laughing, for we're free, we've won
...though battle weary, we fear no harm
...for the piper's trill calls us, to the Mother's waiting arms

Annie could feel herself fading away. After Bethan had brought her home and Harry had bustled around importantly; she remembered wondering why Claire's husband was there, until cognisance filtered in, together with a pang of shame.

She remembered Harry leaving and her neighbour calling in to see if she needed anything. Weakly, she said, 'Thank you for this Eve. My neck hurts and my head, in fact, I feel really strange'; they were the last words she spoke before falling unconscious.

In her deepest state, she relived the moment when a strange creature had fallen toward the bonfire and she had instinctively wanted to save it. It had looked like a brightly shining firefly at first before changing into the creature from a nightmare at her touch. Mabon ...it had been Mabon and already she was behaving strangely, feeling not at all like herself.

She remembered Sybille had left early at Lammas rather than Samhain, without telling her… packing up the shop for a year instead of letting her look after it as usual. Something had been different and then the four young women had arrived and taken over. She remembered how angry she had been with Sybille for not letting her knows what she had planned, but grateful that they gave her work. She had felt so resentful of being dependant on their goodwill and had still behaved so badly toward them.

As her thoughts drifted, she vowed to apologise to them all… and then there was Vanessa; there was another apology to make. What had gotten into her recently that she should have become such a first class bitch? Her neck and face were beginning to ache and she felt sick again. Fancy being sick all over the floor at work, she thought.

Deep within La Stregga stirred restlessly. She could feel Annie's pain as her own and knew something was far from all right. Slowly but surely she had been planting gentle seeds of positive Magick within Annie's psyche; to no avail, the hold the Dark Fae had over the poor woman's vanity was huge.

Now she could feel Annie fading; her mental capacity diminishing as fine inky-black webbing started to move its way across her skin from an obvious puncture wound to her neck. It spread up across one side of her face, probing into ear, nose and eye cavities, seeking brain matter and down, over her shoulder, working its way into lymph nodes in her armpit and under her soft breast tissue until it crawled, inexorably, toward her heart.

From a long way away, Annie heard someone calling her name repeatedly. At first it sounded like Sybille but she realised it came from within herself; the Italian Wytch she thought, who had merged with her a while ago and had fought to help her balance her energies again. Her own arrogance was the price she now paid for her life, which she felt slipping away.

Another voice interceded; pleaded she stay, but the blight, removed by the one she had thought to be her Goddess, who had healed her and restored her to a youthful appearance and vitality, had returned three fold. Annie could feel it eating into her skin and burrowing deep; a bitter taste rose in her mouth. Someone took hold of her hand, warm drops of moisture fell; tears, she realised, her daughter's tears. She gathered every ounce of strength to open her eyes and to touch her daughter's hand; one last time, but the veil was already over her eyes. Annie and La Stregga were floating free, away from earthly ties that bind. Her last conscious thought was that someone was crying. Why was someone crying?

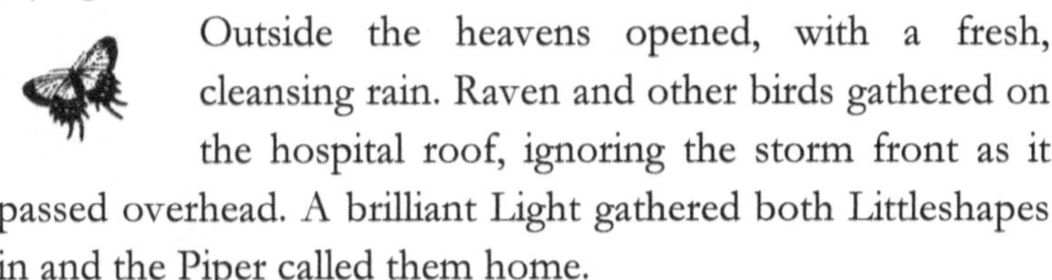 Outside the heavens opened, with a fresh, cleansing rain. Raven and other birds gathered on the hospital roof, ignoring the storm front as it passed overhead. A brilliant Light gathered both Littleshapes in and the Piper called them home.

Chapter 44
Last Tears

...when we travel the Way on the long road of dreams
...through the West portals' shining... across emotional streams
...when we fear we will wander, forever roam
... the moment we cease searching... we are home...
...when we live every moment in the depth of our being
... with eyes open wide... the first time truly seeing
...what we thought was separation from the light of our soul
... was merely illusion... we have always been whole

Vanessa held onto her mother's hand until the nurse had gently taken her into a warm but firm embrace and said it was time to let go.

Flora stood in the corner with Claire, silent and compassionate but dry eyed. Claire was trying to remember when Annie had changed so radically and realised it had been a long time ago, so the 'blight' evident on Annie's skin to all but the 'Onceborn', was not the beginning of the change, merely the catalyst. Her one-time friend had always been a strong and somewhat opinionated woman, but never knowingly cruel and Claire thought, how sad her end had been.

Cause of death, had been classified as Meningitis, gone too long untreated. Symptoms ignored, perhaps such as the memory loss, nausea, loss of appetite and violent headaches being classic to this dreadful illness.

Flora and Claire helped Vanessa to her feet as Harry appeared in the doorway. Calling in to see how Annie was before going to Melbourne, the neighbour had alerted him to Annie's state. He too stood dry eyed, in a state of shock. Rubbing his eyes and blinking he could see, flickering in and out of his vision, black wavy lines appear and disappear on Annie's skin. Exchanging looks with Claire, who merely raised an eyebrow at him; he did not question the doctor's diagnosis of cause of death.

Taking a deep breath, he stroked Annie's hand in a rare show of tenderness and turning to his daughter, tilted her chin up to see her eyes. They were full of grief for her mother, yes, pity for him, yes, but she made no move to console him and pulled back from his touch.

'Give me time,' was all she whispered to him before turning back to her mother's empty body. Kissing her cheek before the nurse covered her face for the last time; those watching were sure they saw Annie smile.

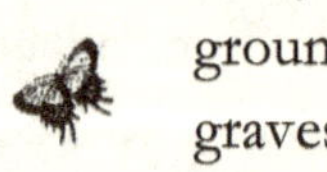

Vanessa brought her mother, Annie Savage, to rest in Springsmeet cemetery, in a part of the wild garden set aside for Pagan folk. Sybille had fought and won a battle years ago that the land be bought and put aside for those who did not follow the Christian tenets …they did not care the ground was 'un-sanctified' in Christian eyes, for every Pagan knows that all of earth is 'hallowed ground'. Unearthly Sounds played a last tribute at her graveside as Vanessa's sweet voice rang out as clear as a bell…

…dawn in the forest as Her Magicks break free… hear Her song on the wind as She stirs an ancient tree. In the depths, in the darkness, where all light is dim… a faint glow can be seen at the edge of sight… on the rim. In your heart, your sense Her as she calls… a soft refrain. In your belly, you feel Her… a flutter… pangs of sweet pain …as your feet take you walking into the depths of Her soft loam …and you'll lay beneath Her fragrant moss… finding home…

Chapter 45

Spring Breaks ...Autumn Arrives

. . . silent the birds . . . still the bees
. . . rivulets of water . . . currents run deep
. . . soon to wake earth from Her long winter sleep
. . . gone longest night and the shortest of days
. . . there's cold still to come, but spring's on Her way
. . . not yet visible, not yet seen
. . . but below the cold ground
. . . the trees thoughts are of green
. . . slowly roots stirring. . . She stretches to wake
. . . drinking in water Her new buds to make
. . . ice and snow forming, but in darkness below
. . . new life awakenings . . . in beauty and flow

Cycles turn on, seasons change and Lammas approached rapidly, mere days away, two years since Sybille had disappeared. Would they ever find her?

Vanessa had recovered her equilibrium and was actively taking over from her mother at work, showing amazing organisational skills. She felt a sense of peace somehow and knew Nina's presence within, kept her strong and resilient; nothing could have been worse than the way Magdalena had died. Vanessa kept an eye on Sam now too, as did the others, realising the pain she must have suffered on all levels of awareness.

Passing through the veil that evening, they gathered at Rob's in Glastonbury, where there was more space than at Lily's little house above the shop, with the land running down to a broad lake and an orchard. Sam always wondered at how similar the landscape was on the other side of the world at Covenstead, the link between the two, energetically obvious. Now little Alma was about to show them the Way; waterways, wells deep underground that linked the worlds, ley lines, song-lines that echoed back and forth between, by which the Fae races made their journeys from Covenstead to Glastonbury and back again as the wheel spun around, especially at Beltane and Samhain.

With each turn of the season and each rite they performed, more Fae gathered to assist as the blight affecting them leaked through the veil and into the earth plane. All of them saw the webbing grow daily and it seemed to have accelerated since Annie's sudden death. The veil had thinned and not thickened again; all manner of creatures, were seen in the surrounding forests at Covenstead. In Glastonbury, wards were renewed nightly and the houses and businesses closed a little earlier, even though Imbolc was close.

They had decided to work in reverse for these Sabbats, Imbolc first to gather in and Lammas to release, but the focus had to be on Lammas as the anniversary of Sybille's disappearance came around.

Tara was rarely seen and Pwyll had again disappeared on his quest to find his wife, but they had agreed to return for the Lammas rite, knowing the importance of having 'all hands on deck' for the working.

Sam had asked Tara about Rowan's bracelet, but Tara knew nothing, every now and again, she sensed Alma and Beth, both knew something about it, but neither would be led to disclose anything and Sam began to feel as if there was some sort of conspiracy going on.

With Rob's guidance and the help of all the shapers, she was beginning to get a grasp of the 'how to' but without the bracelet, the true sense of change eluded her. It was too painful and stressful to go through the change again in reverse and Morgan was fiercely protective when it was suggested.

Now at Imbolc they spent a gentle time calling in the new seeds of change to be harvested the next day at Lammas. How bizarre that they should continually be at both ends of the spectrum at the same time in their parallel travels through the Between. Rob had said they needed to find the fulcrum to balance the shift it took within them in order to maintain their stamina and focus.

They cast a traditional circle that suited the energy of the northern hemisphere's spring arrival. Crocus, bluebells and primroses were beginning to flourish along the lanes and hedgerows; under the canopy of ancient fruit trees, in the orchard, sweet scented blossoms were beginning to open. Still cold, the promise of renewal was strong as they sat around a large bowl of fresh soil, planting their seeds for new growth. Seeds planted in southern hemisphere last Imbolc were now due for harvest in actuality, there and it was for this harvest all their hope was buried in finding the key to returning Sybille home.

Together they chanted a simple rhyme…

We plant these seeds for growth on a waxing moon, may they grow to reward us with this boon that wherever your Priestess Sybille may roam, the Crooked Green Way will guide her safely home.'

They passed the bowl around three times, each of them putting energy into the seeds, watering them in and writing little tags to bury with each one, the words adding direction and focus to the rite.

They were weary, spent and lay beneath the apple trees in a circle, head inwards and holding hands, passing energy to balance them for the Lammas Eve rite to come. Each found they were drifting, anchored to the earth through the roots of the trees and the base of the spine, whilst floating looking down on each other with a mixture of emotions swirling within.

Lily sent love to Max that their relationship could develop and become stable, rooting itself strongly like the willow trees around the lake.

Cal and Flora exchanged energy as the seed of their union grew stronger daily and in silence is renewed vows made only to each other.

Nina stirred within Vanessa, nudging her to take stock of the tiny seed of attraction, sown by the Elflord Aerandir, whose silver-streaked, dark hair lent an air of maturity to otherwise young features. He in turn stood beyond the circle boundaries, standing guard and sensing the young humankin who fascinated him with her guileless innocence.

Claire sat above the grove in a tree, her energy focussed on Pwyll who had arrived briefly and whom she knew would leave just as quickly in his relentless search for answers. Their silent oath to each other was for the time this was all done and no matter the outcome; they would find their way back to renew together.

Alex and Susan sent energy to their children to strengthen their resolve; they knew they were merely backstops in this evolving search for their friend Sybille.

Maeve and Jamie, with little Alma tucked between them sent energy to help with the search before turning to each other. New energy surged between them and Alma grinned at the thought of a little sibling. She knew enough about the cycles to know that it was not that long before the wheel spun on again to Beltane and a new dance would begin for her parents.

Morgan and Sam exchanged energy for her full return to the Ravenkin ancestry, to the end of their long search and for their own awakening feelings, new, yet ancient in the weave.

Aithlin watched his beautiful daughter and his proud nephew as they both grew and matured before his eyes. Strong seeds who would grow strong roots. He looked at Aerandir and Arianwen and saw their mirror image faces… another small seed began to grow tiny roots… something he would have to delve deeply into and in order to do that he would have to help Pwyll find his wife. The more eyes the better, he thought.

Beth grew roots; flowers bloomed as she stretched all her senses to feel Hercurin as he travelled the roadways Between. Here it was planting time, and there it would be harvest within a day's cycle across the physical world. Her seed was firmly planted in renewal, but first there was the job to complete to return Sybille home. Then she would find Circaea and speak of her mother again, spend time with her kin and with her humankin family and friends. She was almost loath to return to a cool Lammas Eve and the ritual sacrifice of the Harvest Lord to come, this year more bittersweet than ever.

Hours flew by as they anchored themselves and renewed their energy from a burgeoning Imbolc energy before returning for a new battle of wits.

Chapter 46 
Lammas in Covenstead

....a new moon smiles in a darkening sky
...she chases wild spirits as the wind blows them by
...a remnant of new... an instant of light
...a moment of stillness in the gathering night
...a new cycle begins... new ideas taking shape
...she smiles on your ventures... from her fragile moon-scape
...sobs and laughter... joy and tears
...the wheel turns on... through the spinning year
...celebrate the seasons... each in their own way
...dance the dance of life... live in the moment every day

With barely time to shower again and change their robes it was the hour for the Lammas rite. Flora swept the circle, focusing all her intent into sweeping away all negativity that might linger there from the events of recent times; Goddess knew there were many.

Jamie and Maeve cast the circle, aware of each other, aware of the bond they shared and of their little girl who waited for them, hidden in a thread in the weave with The Cybil for this evening's work.

'Maeve let go her doubts and spun the energy…

I cast thee oh circle that thou be the boundary between the realms of men and the realms of the Mighty Ones; a guard and protection, which will preserve and contain the energies we do raise within thee, wherefore do I bless and consecrate thee.'

Vanessa, Flora, Beth and Lily called the quarters together, rather than the traditional, individual calling in.

'Guardians of the Watchtowers of the east, north, west and south; of air, fire, water and earth. We do summon and stir thee to witness our rite and to guard this circle.' They each chanted the sound of the four winds of the directions. Alex, Cal, Morgan

and Max stood between each of them, focusing the energy to create an arch of power over the cross-quarters as well as the quarters; it appeared as an eight pointed Elven star, shimmering with energy that beckoned the Fae and the elemental sprites to attend. Aerandir, Aithlin and two more Forest-Fae who had volunteered their energy, stood in the outside cross quarters; four beautiful Fae female-kin had come forward to stand in the quarters.

'*Guardians of the Watchtowers of the north-east, north-west, south-west and south-east of spirit and the energy of Aether that binds them all; we do summon and stir thee to witness this rite and to guard this circle.*' They too intoned a note of summoning.

All the other Grove members entered one by one, circling and spiralling as they chanted a Circle chant of sobbing poignancy…

'*She changes her gown as the year grows old, from russet to amber… green to gold. She's the Lady of the harvest for all living things, in the hedgerows and forests a rich bounty She brings. He changes His cloak as She changes Her gown… they dance at Lammas' hay wain, 'til in sacrifice He's cut down.*

Yet they dance on and on, as the falling leaves twirl, through the mossy glades twilight to the pipes sobbing skirl… that breaks through the silence of a darkening year… then on toward Mabon, the crisp air becomes clear.

On they dance toward Samhain, the ancestors awake and the Wild Hunt comes riding the years' fallen to take, through the veil brightly gleaming, long hair, darkly streaming… and the hound's wild belling, cause the forests to shake.

On and on yet, they dance to Yule's last, long, dark day… the light becomes stronger, yet Jack Frost's still at play… but on they dance toward Imbolc as the first lambs are born… ever onward to bright Ostara, the sun's rays become warm.

Then, when May blossoms open, their honey perfumes the air, step abroad as the sun rises to make a wreath for your hair …for here at the rite of Beltane, their dance flames with bright joy, and folk may later harvest a girl or a boy.

On to Litha they dance, sweet berries flavour the wine… the sun's power reaches zenith and will slowly decline; on the breeze, you'll hear Her singing... in the thunder His rumbling mirth… when they call us, we'll dance with them... in circle spinning... death to rebirth…

They walked the completed circle holding hands, male to female, female to male; raising energy, consciously building a circle of light, while chanting…

'We create a Sacred Space, filled with the love of nature, filled with Light and Hope,' three times. Each in consciousness took a measured step forward toward the centre and sat down.

Jamie and Maeve passed blessed water around to cleanse their energy, smoke for smudging, the altar candle to bring light and a vial of blessed anointing oil in a bowl of water, which was passed around to anoint between their brows… each intoned…

'Bless me Mother for I am your child.'

Then together they sang…

'We strive toward Spirit again and again, with faltering steps, unsure of the Way. Open the Gates of Enlightenment make for us a new day, of purpose toward our goal, a path to a New Earth Soul.'

Standing, they raised their arms, cupping the energy of the Dark Moon; drawing Her down into the self and the circle with the intention to heal.

They drummed, finding a hypnotic rhythm with bells, rattles and pipes; those who didn't play clapped their hands. Raising energy they walked the circle again, chanting…

'East, West, South, North, in Sacred Space we call you forth. Bring Your Power and Your grace, live within our Sacred Place,' three

times.

They wrote what they would sacrifice for Lammas on pieces of paper, folded away from them three times, indicating release and floated in a bowl of water placed in the centre, representing their sacrifice be washed clean as an offering.

They did the same with their goals, each calling out for the energy they needed with a dedication, vowing to take action in a certain way; sharing how they would bring it about through their actions. This time they folded the paper toward them indicating receipt of energy before placing it in another bowl in the centre, amongst carefully chosen seeds; these they would plant in spring for their Imbolc ritual. Nothing ever happens in isolation and all Sabbats are linked.

Grounding the energy in silence, they contemplated the sacrifice of the God of Nature, placing their... hands on the earth and then holding hands again to re-balance.

Bethan fetched bread from the altar, ritually 'stabbing' it to signify the death of the Harvest God before breaking it into pieces for each of them. Breaking hers once, she said…

'Maiden Goddess, keep me whole, let your beauty fill my soul,' before eating the piece, savouring every morsel. Breaking it a second time she chanted…

'Mother, Goddess, keep me whole; let your power fill my soul.' This one she dipped in salt and ate, then with the last piece dipped in salt and seeds she chanted…

'Crone Goddess, keep me whole, let your wisdom fill my soul,' before eating this too. She passed everything sunwise and the ritual was repeated by each of the Grove. Once again, they held hands to re-centre the energy into cohesion.

They all felt the shift in Sam the moment she had completed her ritual; last in the circle. Beth shifted and changed as Arianwen stepped into the circle centre, holding out the silver bracelet to Sam. 'It's time sister; it's your time to fly.'

Sam's head swam as if she had downed a bottle of mead; reaching for the bracelet that would change everything for her and enable her to fly with her kin to finally bring Sybille home… too late, the change came upon her violently and rapidly and she spun out of control, her body wracked with the excruciating process of the reverse change. Sam embraced the dark… another thread spun out to join with all those, affecting the weave of the tangled silken web…

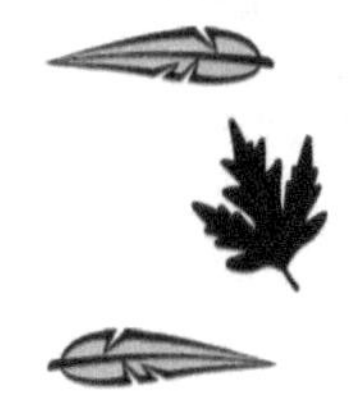

Epilogue
Rowan

...raven flight ...wings of inky quills
...a fragile span that time spills
...into the warp and weft of pain
...searching the Aethers for an iota of gain
...to numb the feeling that all is lost
...for only the smallest quota
...of consciousness remains
...lost in a silken web of a Raven's bane

As Rowan lost consciousness, in the final descent, all she could see was the black interior behind her eyes; she was falling again, lost and disorientated. She felt herself shrinking, failing in strength; her last conscious thought was, 'I'm dying... this cannot be.' She screamed feebly, '... but I'm one of the Mother's Magicks I'm immortal. Ruark,' she screamed again '... where's Ruark.' Her physical shell, torn by arrows fell to the earth.

Contrary to all the rules of Magicks, she brought together enough energy to curse aloud the one who was her end. Her body, twisted out of all recognisable shape, her tears fell to earth black and sticky, blighting the lands Between and all that would encounter it, she screamed, her cry becoming the guttural caw of her kind...

'I bind you to eternal dark, I will return to make my mark. In truth, I curse you for your guile; believe you've won for just a while. For I curse you to live in the in-between, your voice to be heard, yet you remain unseen; forever in darkness, never free... as I do will so mote, it be.'

As Rowans words echoed through the Skeins, they rebounded as all negative Magicks do, striking all and any who haplessly travelled the roadway Between.

Her physical eyes dimmed and filmed over, staring sightlessly; she was lost, falling, a spark of light that darkened as it fell, knocking into a cocoon on the Tree of Birthing, tearing it free of its threads and plunging its occupant into an unconscious void.

Touching a woman named Jennifer with her sting; she died just mere weeks later of a rare and strange cancer of the blood. Causing the death of a man named Richard, a good man who would never have taken his own life, despite the grief for his wife. It brushed past a small child, allowing one with negative Magick the energy to transform sticks and leaves to create a fetch so that she could steal a child away. Even to halt an attempt to save the same child from drowning and to let a Dark Fae kill another Fae spirit as she gave birth on a lakeshore. On and on the Darkmaker fell altering and changing all she touched with her Magick gone awry… one of the Mother's little Magicks was lost.

Before the realisation could fully hit Sybille that she was renewing, she felt herself ripped from her physical body.

On Rowan fell towards earth, where a spark of light flickered, calling her with subtle guile.

'Come, we can help you,' called the Salamanders of flame.

'Come we can help you,' called the Sylphs of Air as they blew the smoke upwards and fed the flames.

'Come we can heal you,' cried the Dryads of the trees as their branches, sacrificed to the Salamander's fire sought fuel that they may burn longer.

A scream of terror ripped through the Between as Magdalena faced the fire and a cauldron of water in Maeve's studio came by itself to boiling, rumbling and bubbling before bursting up in a geyser.

'Come we can help you,' screamed the water Merrow, 'you can find peace and heal your corruption in the cleansing pools of the depths of us.'

Rowan heard nothing more as she fell deeper still toward the flame. Her vision cleared a little as she saw the female standing on the edge of the forest, her face a mask of hatred, bearing a puckered scar on one cheek. Her she cried, Aelish Farandirim, the cause of her death and with a small cry plummeted willingly toward the flames.

Annie Savage stepped forward to catch the little spark she saw falling toward the flames, trying to make sense of what it was; a firefly perhaps? A dim memory surfaced of an elder wytch who was trying to warn her of a pending disaster, but the small creature panicked, growing a spiked tail and tattered wings and in a last attempt to save herself, stung Annie in the neck.

A tall Dark Fae came out of the forest, moving fast. He caught her and she clung, shrinking in fear to his shoulder as he carried her away into the forest.

...to be continued in the final episode...
Silver's Threads Book 5, Skeins of Tyme...

Penny Reilly Author 2014

About the Author

Renowned as a clairvoyant and a teacher of the Western Mysteries at Daylesford School of Arcane Knowledge, Penny Reilly is an initiated Bard in the Tradition of the Druid. Moving on this year to the Order of Ovate, Penny has a passion for the Old Ways of the British Isles; she will be returning there this year to carry out research for her nonfiction books and her second 'Cloak of Magick' series to come. She feels that the gentle path of the Druid, Pagan-Wytchways is the path to take for a sustainable future, connecting us to the land, no matter where we live on the planet. She describes herself as a 'nature writer'.

Her own visionary experiences are very much a part of her storyline, poetry and lyrics …this is her fourth published book. She has previously written articles for alternative magazines, blogs regularly about her ideas and way of life, writes for 'starts at sixty' lifestyle blog and has over 5,000 followers on her poetry page 'earthly rites', her school and her author page on Facebook.

Penny moved to Sydney, Australia in 1980 and to the central highlands of Victoria with her husband David, 18 years ago. They share space with an 'all sorts' terrier, an old tabby cat, a small flock of hens and a fat wombat fondly known as 'Chocolat', who has adopted them. Keen gardeners, they are becoming self-sufficient on their beautiful rolling acres on the Great Divide; their blended mob of children are long 'grown and flown' the coop.

You can find out more about the author, her books, poetry, tours and workshops, through her website, amazon.com and social media pages

http://silversthreads.wordpress.com/
http://amazon.com/pennyreilly
http://facebook.com/pennyreillyauthorpage
http://facebook.com/earthlyrites
http://facebook.com/daylesfordschoolofarcaneknowledge
http://www.goodreads.com/pennyreilly